ANDERLOSS

RACE TO ANDERLOSS

Lynette Bishop

Scripture Union
130 City Road London EC1V 2NJ

By the same author:
Escape from Gehalla
The Key of Zorgen

© Lynette Bishop 1992
First published 1992

ISBN 0 86201 755 6

British Library Cataloguing-in-Publication Data.
A catalogue record for this book is available from the British
Library.

Phototypeset by Intype, London
Printed and bound in Great Britain by Cox and Wyman Ltd,
Reading

Chapter one

Alex walked through the door of the space shuttle like someone passing the point of no return. There was one empty seat in the small circle of padded recliners waiting for him. He eased his long frame into it and snapped the seat-belt round his waist. Behind him the door of the shuttle slammed shut. Sealed in! He glanced round at the faces of his five companions and saw that they were as tense as he was.

The engines roared into life and Alex felt his pulses quicken. The shuttle zoomed into orbit. A surge of excitement swept through him like an electric shock. The race was about to begin.

All contact with Base was now broken. Later, when Alex left the shuttle, he would be completely on his own. There would be radio contact with the other competitors but Alex wondered how much use that would be. He wasn't sure if they could really trust each other when each of them wanted to win.

Alex knew how desperately he himself wanted to win. It seemed as if all his life had led up to this race. The prize, a place in the SESU – the Space Explorers' Special Unit – was what he wanted more than anything else in his whole life. Now the training was over. All the elimination rounds which he had survived meant nothing. Everything hung on the events of the next few hours.

'It doesn't matter if you lose, Alex,' his father had said. 'God has a plan for your life. This may not be it. You have many gifts and talents. The SESU might be the right place for you to use them. Or you might be better off using them somewhere else.'

A surge of anger swept through Alex as he remembered his father's words. He was proud of his father in some ways. He was a good man, a fair man, respected by everyone in the growing community on Reba, the isolated district in the north-west sector where Alex had grown up. Alex's father was leader of the community but, even so, Alex felt that his father was a failure. The north-west sector was virtually uninhabited. What did being a leader count for where there were hardly any people? He had heard it said that his father was all set for a brilliant career, but something had happened and instead he was stuck in a backwater, doing a job that anyone could have done with their eyes closed.

Alex had never been able to discover the full story, but he was sure that part of the problem was his father's misplaced belief in this unseen, vague being he called God. It was his way of getting out of facing up to things. Alex had come to a firm belief of his own. What happened to you in this life was up to you. There was nobody and nothing to help you but yourself. There was no way Alex was going to be a loser like his father. He was determined to win this race.

Coming out of his reverie, Alex found he was gripping the arm-rests of his seat as if his life depended on it. A cold sweat had broken out on his forehead.

'Hey, relax, man!' The cheerful voice jarred and Alex glared at the speaker lounging in the seat opposite. 'It's only a race. The worst that can happen is that you'll lose. Either that or be gobbled up by a hairy monster.'

All six competitors had spent the final week of training together. After that they felt they'd seen some of the worst as well as the best sides of each other. Ricky's non-stop cheerfulness and stream of unfunny jokes had been almost harder to take than the rigours of training.

Ricky's light-brown eyes sparkled as he beamed round at the others. 'Anyone feel like a last Coke? We can always press the emergency button and have you dropped back in to Base.' He glanced at the five unsmiling faces around him. 'No takers?' he asked, raising his sandy eyebrows in surprise.

'Pack it in,' grunted Seth, his usual brusque self.

Ricky shrugged his shoulders. 'OK,' he said, smiling evenly. 'Keep cool.'

The shuttle was travelling smoothly. The pre-set controls were working normally. It was a routine journey, though the destination was a little out of the ordinary. Alex had heard of the Waste Zone, had studied maps, read up on it and watched the latest video of it, but he had never been there. It looked a desolate place. The rumours were that although it was uninhabited there was some kind of danger, unspecified but hinting at a hidden menace. Still, he would be glad to get there, glad to get the first test over and be working on his own.

They all sat in silence watching the dials, the flashing red and green lights on the switchboard. They were waiting for the orange light that would signal the start of the race. Alex sat staring for so long he was afraid he wouldn't see it when it finally did light up. But he saw it immediately and his heartbeat quickened. As soon as it came on, Jeff, cool and self-contained, rose to his feet.

'Time to begin, I think,' he said.

There were six computers on the upper deck of the shuttle. Each competitor had a coloured tag corresponding to a coloured button on one of the computers. Each computer had the same programme, testing the quickness and ingenuity of the competitors. But the final instructions, which had to be decoded, were different in each case. Each gave the location of a spaceship which contained a flag of the same colour as the tags and computer buttons. A slim electronic device lay on the surface next to the computer which would be used later to open the spaceship door. The ultimate winner of the race would be the first to place his flag on the summit of Anderloss Mountain in the heart of the Waste Zone.

Of all the stages of the race, Alex expected this first stage to be the most difficult for him. When it came to the stamina and ingenuity he would need later he expected to make up some ground on the others. But even in this initial test he hoped to gain third place.

Alex quickly located his computer but, as he made his way over to it, he almost collided with Ben who was gazing in bewilderment round the room.

'No orange . . .' he began.

'Watch where you're going,' said Alex abruptly. 'And don't ask for help,' he added impatiently. 'This is supposed to be a race.'

He slipped into his seat at his computer. He turned to Ben before examining the controls. 'At least you'll know yours is the only one left when everyone else sits down,' he said – then felt guilty when Ben smiled gratefully. No time to think of anyone else, he told himself. Just concentrate if you want to win.

Finally, he sat back with a sigh of satisfaction. He had completed the programme and had the location of his spaceship. He rubbed his neck and stretched, looking round the room to see who was still left. He had been vaguely aware of Jeff getting up some time back. But he had expected that. Where would cool, calculating Jeff succeed but with the computer? Now he saw that Seth had gone. That was no surprise either. Seth, he had quickly realised, was big-headed and ruthless with it. If it was possible to cheat, he felt sure Seth would have done it. But he hadn't expected Ricky to be gone. Maybe the clowning around was only one side of Ricky.

He was sure he would catch up if he hurried. He walked briskly across the room, passing the last two competitors engrossed in their computers. Ben had obviously found his orange-buttoned computer. Alex couldn't understand how someone as hesitant as Ben could have secured a place as one of the six finalists in the race. But then none of them knew each other very well. Anyway, even poor Ben shouldn't come last. They all knew who would be last.

The sixth competitor, bent intently over the red computer, was a girl. Callie was the first girl to gain a place in the race. She seemed full of self-confidence as she swung her plait of fair hair back over her shoulders. But the others smiled behind her back. Yes, thought Alex, at least Ben didn't have to worry about coming last.

The Waste Zone was as bleak as he had imagined. Despite the warm, protective suit he wore, with its insulated, thermal jacket, the cold air hit him as he stepped out of the shuttle. He realised he should have kept an eye on the others to assess how big a start they had on him. That was his first mistake. He must be careful to keep his wits about him now and make sure that it was his last. He set his electronic compass for the destination where his spaceship would be waiting. Then he looked around him, trying to remember all he had seen and heard about this strange place.

It was a grey and rocky landscape, completely unrelieved by any landmarks except for the craggy cliffs which rose precipitously to his left and a crater which tore a gash through the flat land to his right, hedged on the skyline by a semicircle of high rocks. Ahead the land was flat, broken here and there by scrubby vegetation, stunted trees, the occasional outcrop of rocks and shallow craters. But it was impossible to see very far because of the curtain of dust which masked much of the light and made the whole landscape dark and gloomy.

Alex whistled softly to himself and took a few steps forward in the direction indicated by the compass, feeling he must move straight away before he lost the confidence to move at all.

He had no idea now of how far ahead the others were if their paths were set in different directions. He shivered as the thought came to him that he was unlikely to see anyone again until the race was over and he was safely back at Base. Well, that was what he had wanted, wasn't it? To be on his own? Of course there was always radio contact with the others, but that was only for emergencies. Alex did not imagine he would have any use for that.

It was certainly different from home! He smiled wryly at the thought as he strode along as briskly as he dared in the uncertain terrain. And that was what he wanted too. That was why he was in this race. To be different. His parents lived such ordinary lives in the small community at Reba, where nothing changed from one year to the next. He wanted the chance to prove that he could do something special, rise above the ordinary.

The SESU certainly offered that – exploring new territories, pioneering, discovering new planets and new places where people could settle and make a better way of life. His thoughts were forced back to the grey wilderness which had wrapped itself round him in an eerie silence. As uninhabited places go, not my number one choice, he thought.

At first it seemed like an adventure. But after a while the monotony of the landscape and the heaviness of the misty, grey air dampened his enthusiasm. He felt as if he had been walking for hours. Despite all the training his feet had begun to ache, his limbs felt heavy, and the pack on his back felt as if it was full of the small rocks that were strewn across his path. He felt quite hot as he walked along but if he stopped to rest, the freezing cold bit into him immediately.

Come on, he told himself. Stamina's the thing you're supposed to have most of. His mind went briefly to the other competitors, wondering how they were managing. He grimaced as he thought of Ben and Callie trying to cope on their own. He shook his head. Concentrate, he told himself. That's what this race is all about – trying to succeed where others fail. Nobody needs to win as badly as I do.

A renewed determination to beat the others gave him a fresh burst of energy. He strode more quickly over the rocky terrain, picturing himself arriving at Anderloss Mountain, climbing to the top and planting his flag.

The shrill noise, shattering the deathly silence of the Waste Zone, startled him. His mouth went dry with sudden fear before he realised that it was the signal of his own radio. The beating of his pulse steadied as he reached to press the button on his wrist console, but a feeling of deep unease persisted. He cleared his throat and forced himself to speak into the microphone. His voice sounded strange and hoarse to his own ears. 'Code Green Three here,' he said. 'Come in.'

Chapter two

The radio crackled and Alex strained to make out the sound of a voice. The only sound coming over the line was that of heavy interference. Alex's feeling of foreboding deepened. He spoke into the microphone again.

'Code Green Three. I'm not getting anything. Can you speak louder?'

This time the interference did not seem so bad but, hard as he listened, Alex could not make out the suspicion of a voice. He was about to speak into the microphone again when he thought he caught the sound of a word. He listened intently and this time he was able to distinguish the word, 'Help.' Alex's heart sank in dismay. Who was it that was calling and what had happened to them that was making them seek help?

'Code Green Three. I can hear you, but only just. Give me your name, position and reason for requiring help.'

Alex waited with bated breath as the crackling came through the miniature radio on his wrist console again. Now he was beginning to feel desperate. How could he help whoever it was if he could not hear them clearly? Meanwhile time was ticking away when he needed every second to catch up with the other competitors.

He had almost decided that he must switch off the console when the crackling suddenly stopped and a voice came through. It was faint, unrecognisable, but the words came clearly enough.

'Alex! Alex, help me! Can't . . . hold on . . .'

The words ended in an abrupt cry of fear and pain. Alex spoke quickly into the microphone. 'Hold on! I'm coming. Just tell me where you are.'

The crackling was beginning again but Alex caught the faint words '. . . three trees . . . dragon stone . . . Alex, quickly!' The awful groan and gasp of terror chilled Alex. As the crackling drowned out the terrified voice, Alex switched to the microphone and spoke urgently.

'I don't understand. Give the reference of your location or I won't be able to find you.'

He switched to the speaker again, ready to strain to hear the smallest fragment of information over the noise of crackling. To his dismay, instead of the terror-stricken voice or even the frustrating crackling of interference, there was nothing to be heard at all. The radio was dead. Whoever had been calling him urgently was no longer there.

Three trees. Dragon stone.

That was all the information he was left with. He was not even sure that he had heard correctly. Without any directions how could he hope to find the location? The Waste Zone covered a vast area. Someone leaving the space shuttle at roughly the same time as Alex, but moving in a different direction, could be absolutely anywhere.

Thinking of the others reminded Alex of the urgency of the race. The other competitors, moving ahead steadily, would reach Anderloss Mountain before Alex. No one else had had this delay. Except, of course, the person who had signalled so urgently for help.

Alex was torn. No race, surely, was worth leaving someone facing fear and pain, perhaps even in danger of their life. Alex felt he had no choice but to search for the three trees and the dragon stone.

Alex looked around him, hoping for some clue as to which direction he should strike out in. He might as well, he supposed, go forward, following his own compass reading and hope that he would see a cluster of trees or a stone shaped like a dragon.

Once the decision was made, Alex moved quickly ahead but, instead of feeling at ease with his choice of action, he was surprised to find himself feeling more and more unsettled as he walked on. Adding to the question of whether he was doing the right thing, came a new, alarming thought. What if the whole thing was a hoax? What if someone was trying to delay him and send him on a wild-goose chase? If that was so, then would there be more tricks to follow? On the other hand, if one of the others really was in danger and Alex was the only person they could contact, how would he feel if something happened to them while he selfishly carried on with the race?

It was so unfair. Alex suddenly felt hard done by. There were enough difficulties to face in the race as it was, without this extra, uncalled-for distraction. He determined then that, unless he saw three trees or a dragon-shaped rock fairly soon, he would just concentrate on making the fastest progress he could in the race.

He had gone no more than a few yards when he saw them. Glancing casually to his left, he saw three gnarled, stunted trees on the horizon. He stopped dead in his tracks and, for a moment, he merely stared, thrown again into indecision.

15

'Alex, help,' the voice had pleaded. 'Alex, quickly!' Then there had come the awful cries of fear and pain. Before he could change his mind, Alex left his compass path and set off steadily across country to the three trees.

There was no sign of anyone else about, no sound or movement apart from his own light tread across the dusty, rock-strewn ground. Even so, as he neared the trees, Alex slowed down, straining to catch a sound. There was nothing. No whimpering cry of pain or whispered call for help. No sound of someone and something lying in wait. No suspicion of hidden danger.

A low outcrop of rocks lay to one side of the open ground between Alex and the trees. Alex moved swiftly to the rocks and then cautiously in their shadow until he had a closer view of the trees. None of the rocks he skirted was even remotely shaped like a dragon. There were no other rocks within the vicinity of the trees which could fit that description either. But, in this landscape of rock, crater and scrub, trees were unusual. Three together were rare. This must be the place. The question was, what had happened to whoever it was who had made that call for help? Did the same danger lie in wait for Alex beyond those twisted trees?

He listened intently as he moved. His hand went to the laser gun at his side, ready to draw it at the first sign of danger. He heard nothing. He saw no-one. With a sigh of relief he reached the small band of trees. It was only when he actually came up to the trees that he saw, to his surprise, that the land beyond them was not flat. It dropped away abruptly at the edge of the trees to an unseen gully.

Alex gasped in astonishment at the sight which met his eyes as he peered over the edge. The sides of the gully were studded with prickly bushes and clumps of scrub, flourishing to a greater extent in this sheltered pocket of land than on the dust-blown surface. Half-way down the gully, on a patch of earth bare of bushes and scrub, there was a rock. Once the suggestion had been made to you, you could see quite clearly that it was shaped like a small, crouching dragon.

The surprise of finding not only the three trees but the dragon rock was almost immediately replaced by another feeling – that his being here was a mistake. The gully had the air of a place undisturbed by human presence. There was no sign of anyone ever having set foot in this hidden place.

Even as Alex began scrambling down the slope towards the dragon rock, he began to feel sure that he would find no one here now. He stopped suddenly and the grey dust rose in small clouds where his booted feet had skidded to a halt. If there was no one here then the call had been a trick. And if that were true then Alex was doing exactly what the unknown hoaxer wanted him to do. He was walking into a trap. That was his last amazed thought as a disturbance from the slope above sent a cascade of small rocks and stones sweeping down the slope behind him, making him lose his footing. To his horror he found himself hurtling helplessly down the slope. The dark shape of the dragon rock loomed nearer as he rolled and twisted downwards, scrabbling vainly with his hands to grasp at a branch of bush or scrub.

The grey sky tilted into grey soil. The three trees stretched gnarled limbs as if to push him downwards faster into the waiting jaws of the dragon rock. Then, miraculously, his bruised hand clasped the rough wood of a dolomite bush. Relief flooded through him. Alex looked upwards for a second hand-hold and thought briefly that he saw a shadow move against the grey sky. Then, without warning, the branch in his hand snapped and he went plummeting downwards towards the dragon rock. His head cracked against something with a swift, blinding pain and the grey world became suddenly black.

Chapter three

Something was clawing at Alex, digging into him, scratching him. It seemed as if his skull had been cracked open and the nerve ends were being teased with red-hot pincers. Slowly, warily, Alex opened his eyes. Light dazzled him. A new pain began throbbing behind his eyelids. He closed his eyes quickly again and groaned. He tried to move his right hand. Whatever it was that held him dug deeper into his skin. He cried aloud at the intensity of pain and his eyelids flew open again.

There was no one torturing him. His fall had been broken by a prickly dolomite bush, larger and sturdier than the one whose branch had snapped earlier in his hand. It was the thick thorns which studded the flower-bearing branches that were digging into him. He must have hit his head against the scaly trunk as he had fallen.

The good thing about the situation was that the dolomite bush had saved him from dashing his brains out on the dragon rock. The problem was that it had also trapped him. Thorns pinned his arms and legs to the bush. He dared not move.

Strangely enough, though he was in an almost impossible predicament, Alex felt no sense of panic. Trying to stay on top of the pain left little room for fear. There had to be a way of getting out of this and safely back on to his original course. All he had to do was to try and think clearly through the red haze of pain.

The way he had fallen, most of his weight had pushed his right side into the bush. His right arm and leg were pinned beneath him against the thorny branches, but his left hand was only trapped because the sleeve of his jacket was caught on the thorns.

Very gingerly he flexed his fingers, easing his hand into a space between branches free from thorns. Experimentally he pulled his arm. With a tearing sound, it came free of the imprisoning branch above it, but the effort left him gasping with pain as the weight on his right side shifted, thrusting him deeper on to the thorns beneath him. For a few minutes he lay as still as possible, automatically taking deep breaths to ride the pain as he had been taught to do in training. At last, the pain subsided to a dull throbbing and he turned his attention back to his left arm. To his amazement he found that the first pull had jerked it completely free. After that it was just a question of slow, agonising movement to ease first his left leg, then his right side free of the thorns. When it was done, he rolled over on to his back and lay exhausted on the bare slope of the gully.

It was some time later before Alex was able to complete the climb out of the gully. He groped in his backpack for a medi-capsule to ease the pain and for ointment to rub into the many cuts and bruises. He also swallowed a vitamin and glucose capsule, forcing himself to rest while his reserves of energy built up.

The rigorous training he had undergone over the past few months now stood him in good stead. Despite the cold, he would have liked to have been able just to lie still, as movement immediately brought twinges of pain to his stiff limbs. It was the long hours of disciplined training which now helped him to get up and carry on.

He had lost, he estimated, between twenty minutes and half an hour. Not so very long compared to the time he could have lost if he had fallen further down the gully, or if he had injured himself more seriously in the fall. It would be difficult to make up the time and catch up with the three boys in the lead. But it was not impossible.

After several minutes of steady walking, it seemed the medicine and ointment were working to good effect, for Alex found he could increase his speed. He felt a new surge of energy and a growing sense of confidence as he drew nearer to the towering range of craggy cliffs which he had seen in the distance when he had left the space shuttle. All the same he would be glad to arrive at the stopping place indicated on the digital map on his wrist console.

Alex was glancing at the console when the signal on his radio shrilled, shattering the silence. He almost jumped and stared at the console as the radio continued to bleep impatiently, demanding his attention. A cold finger of fear touched him. The memory of the unidentified voice crying, begging for help, came clearly back – the voice which had lured Alex into danger. Then he remembered the shadow he thought he had glimpsed at the top of the gully. Uneasily he looked around him, half expecting to see someone watching him now. There was no one.

The radio continued its shrill bleeping. Alex's hand hovered over the button which would allow him to speak into the microphone. The thought came to him suddenly that if someone was trying to sabotage the race, if they were setting another trap, then he now had a weapon with which to fight them. He knew what they were up to. He could try and catch them out.

In a mood of defiance he spoke briskly into the microphone. 'Code Green Three here. Come in.'

This time there was no crackling. The voice came clearly but hesitantly. 'Alex? Is that you? It's Ben here.'

Alex felt a rush of disappointment. It was only Ben. At Ben's next words his heart sank. Ben's voice was breathless and strained. 'Alex, I need help. Can you come?'

Alex sighed. Though he felt like screaming with frustration, he forced himself to say, 'Code Green Three here. Please use your code, Ben. State your location and your problem.'

'Look, I don't think I can hold on,' came Ben's voice, edged with pain. 'You set out just before me. I think you must be the nearest, Alex. Can you come quickly? Please?'

Alex thought of the recent crisis he had gone through himself. He had coped without having to delay any of the other competitors by asking for help. Probably Ben's problem was something he was perfectly capable of sorting out himself if he wasn't so weak-willed. Alex lost control. 'For goodness sake, Ben, what's wrong?' he snapped into the microphone.

He felt immediately remorseful as the voice came back subdued. 'Sorry. I've fallen and got my leg caught in some kind of a trap. I don't think I can get it free without help. I'm not thinking too clearly. It's a bit painful.'

Alex bit his lip, aware of time passing, aware of time he had already lost caught in a trap similar to the one Ben was in now.

'If you head back to the space shuttle, I'm not very far,' Ben was saying.

Back to the space shuttle! thought Alex. Back over all this ground he had covered so painfully – and then to have it to do again! But did he really have any choice? It was what his father would have done without hesitation. Gone back. But then his father wasn't the kind of person who won races – or anything else.

The answer to the problem suddenly came to him. It was so simple he wondered why he hadn't thought of it before. 'Look, Ben,' he said, 'isn't Callie nearer to you . . . ?'

'Yes,' interrupted the voice, fainter now, 'but I don't know if she could lift this. You're the nearest one who can help me, Alex.'

'Ben, I've set my compass. If I come back I'll have to reset it.' The thought of the long, weary hours of walking that would have to be done again hit him like a physical pain. He would lose so much more time. He supposed he would have to do it. Then came another flash of inspiration. 'Listen, Ben. Are you there?'

The voice came back faintly and, Alex thought later, hopelessly. 'Ben, try using your laser gun to cut through the area round your leg. Ease yourself free, rest, then see if you can carry on. If not, forget the race and make your way back to the shuttle. I'll let Base know when I get back.'

'OK.' The faint voice did not sound convinced. Alex had a sinking feeling in his stomach. Perhaps he should go after all. It was so cold. Ben, sitting or lying trapped, would freeze.

'Listen,' he said slowly, 'if you try the laser and it doesn't work, call me again and I'll come.'

Alex set off again with Ben's quiet agreement ringing in his ears. He wondered if it was worth pressing on if, in a few minutes, he might have to retrace his steps again. Wouldn't he be better off sitting and resting? But sitting and resting made him think of Ben in the bitter cold, struggling with his laser gun. He was half tempted to retrace his steps then and there.

But he'll probably do it, Alex thought. I managed to get free. Ben will too. I've lost enough time already talking to him. If I went back I'd lose more time for nothing.

It seemed the most sensible idea to set off again, walking quickly, trying not to think of anything but getting to his goal.

There was no further communication from Ben. Time seemed to pass more slowly now and Alex began to tire again. The thought had occurred to him that he ought to forgo the break at the suggested stopping-place so that he could make up for lost time but, as he battled on through the cold, grey landscape, the thought of warmth, rest and food soon became the only thing which kept him going.

The course of Alex's journey had for some time taken him along the line of the cliffs. He paused now in the shelter of an overhang and fished out of his pack a small, slim oblong of shiny metal. On the reverse side was a small screen with a space underneath to slip in a thin plastic card. He had a set of cards, each with a map of a different section of the Waste Zone. He selected the one he wanted and slipped it under the screen. The screen lit up and the map was magnified. Alex studied it closely for several minutes, checking the bearings with his compass reading, before slipping it back into the pack.

He knew now exactly where he was going so he set off briskly, trying to get warm, for in those few minutes the chill had penetrated him to the bone. For a fleeting second he thought of Ben. It occurred to him for the first time that Ben had not called back, not because he was free but because he had passed out from the pain and cold. Well, it was a long time since they had talked. Too late to go back now.

Alex was not thinking of Ben but of the others, wondering how far they had got, when another thought struck him. He stopped abruptly. He could not believe he had been so stupid. Had he been so busy concentrating on stamina that his brain had gone to sleep! How could he hope to qualify for a top intelligence unit like the SESU if it took him this long to think of something so obvious? Ben had not contacted him, but he could contact Ben! It would be such a relief to know that he was all right.

His fingers fumbled with the buttons in his eagerness to use his radio. This time he did not give a second thought to protocol. 'Ben!' he yelled into the microphone, 'Ben, are you there?'

Almost immediately a voice answered. Alex breathed a sigh of relief. It was only when he began to listen to what the voice was saying that his relief turned to bewilderment.

'Get off the line!' the voice was saying sharply. 'Whoever that is, will you get off this line!'

Alex was about to protest when the voice was interrupted by the familiar loud crackling noise of interference. He grimaced and switched the radio off. He immediately became aware of the intense silence around him.

The Waste Zone.

Alex shivered. Ahead the grey landscape stretched away, unnaturally still, to the horizon. To his left the towering cliff-face loomed menacingly over him. There was a strangeness about the whole place which added to his growing sense of unease. It was not as it should be. The race itself was not as it should have been either. This was not what Alex had trained for. It seemed to him in that moment of absolute stillness, with the harsh, threatening voice of some unknown person ringing in his ears, that this race was impossible. There was something peculiar happening which he felt completely inadequate to deal with. He had been putting all the effort he could into making progress in this race, but perhaps he was making no real progress at all. Perhaps he was walking, like a night creature dazzled by bright light, into some sort of trap.

Chapter four

Alex's pulse quickened for a moment. Memories, sharpened by fear, of the painful experience which had begun last time with a crackling on his radio, came flooding back. With an effort he pulled himself together. This incident was altogether different from the one before. All that had happened now was that his radio signal had somehow got mixed up with someone else's. He had heard the understandable angry voice of a person whose conversation had been interrupted. As for the first radio call, that had been an isolated incident. Alex could think of no comfortable explanation for what had happened. It seemed almost certain that someone had set a trap for him. There was nothing he could do now except to stay on the alert.

He increased his pace, moving steadily forward round the rugged contours of the cliff. He was annoyed with himself for the way he was over-reacting. The difficulties he had faced so far were nothing compared with what he would have to deal with if he became a member of the SESU. He was hardly fit to qualify if he could not at least complete this race. Even his father would handle the situation more capably than he was doing. If he was going to stand any chance of winning, Alex had to do much better than he had been doing and he had better start now.

He would begin by trying his radio again. He paused in a sheltered angle of rock and checked the frequency in case it had been wrong the first time he had tried to contact Ben. Again the high-pitched noise of interference shattered the silence. He flicked it off, deciding to waste no more time over Ben, and set off briskly again.

However, as he walked, the puzzle of the unknown voice nagged at him. It was certainly not Ben, but it could have been any of the other three boys. Whoever it was, why had he been so anxious to keep the line clear? Who had he been talking to, and how had Alex tapped into the conversation when he had been trying to reach Ben? If, on top of all this, Alex began asking questions about the earlier phone call, that cry for help which had turned out to be a hoax, then he found himself facing a disturbing and perhaps dangerous situation.

Alex could feel the tension beginning to build up again. These questions were getting him nowhere. He renewed his determination not to let the incident affect him, and turned his thoughts to the stopping-place. He was very eager to get there now. At least it was a place that was mapped out and known in this grey wilderness.

He knew from the compass reading when he at last reached the right spot, though, looking closely at the map, he could not imagine why it had been picked for a stopping-place. There was no obvious shelter. The high walls of the cliff stretched endlessly with rocks and pitted with craters. He moved along the foot of the cliff, trying to pinpoint the exact spot marked on the map. The prospect of not finding anything and having to press on until he reached the spaceship filled him with gloom. The possibility that he would not even complete the race, let alone catch the others up, gripped him with sudden dismay. There had been too many setbacks! Maybe when he got to his special location he wouldn't be able to find his spaceship either.

It was then that he saw something that knocked all other thoughts out of his mind. He had reached a curve in the cliff face where the grey dust which swirled over the surface of the Waste Zone lay settled and undisturbed. Except, very clearly marked in the dust, there were footprints.

The feeling of unease which had come to Alex when he had heard the unknown voice on the radio came back sharply. He thought of the cry for help which had been a trap, and of the suspicion of a shadow at the top of the gully. Of course the logical explanation was that one of the others had come to the same spot. But the footprints seemed to disappear into the rock face.

As Alex rounded the corner, he caught his breath. Set back into the curve of the rock and screened from his side by the contour of the cliff was a narrow opening, scarcely wide enough for one person to squeeze through. He checked his map and found that it corresponded exactly with the spot marked as a stopping-place. However, he hesitated. He had an uneasy feeling about this place. Perhaps it was because of the other things that had happened to him since he had left the space shuttle. Perhaps the unknown voice, luring him to the accident in the gully, had made him suspect danger where it did not exist! But now he felt reluctant to face whoever might be in the hidden place beyond the narrow opening.

Instead of the absolute darkness he had expected, a

pale, luminous, blue light outlined the curve of a tunnel, a low ceiling and an uneven floor. Alex moved slowly and quietly. The coldness of the air now had a frosty chill and the quality of silence seemed to have changed here in this damp place. It was almost as if something lay in the depths of the earth, waiting, holding its breath.

When the light grew brighter, Alex knew he must be nearing the end of the tunnel. He flattened himself back against the wall and edged his way round the last bend, straining to glimpse what lay beyond. As he had half-expected, it was a huge cavern, and it was completely empty.

Alex breathed a sigh of relief as he stepped into the cavern. Apparently, whoever had been here ahead of him had already gone. He looked round and shivered. It was not his idea of a stopping-place. He would eat some of his rations and move on.

He was sitting with his hands cupped round a beaker of warm choc-o-milk, enjoying the heat it gave out, when he became aware of a faint sound coming from beyond the cavern. He hastily gathered his things into his pack and in a matter of seconds was on his feet, ready to move. He tightened his lips, annoyed with himself. He should have walked round the cavern, checking every inch of it, before he sat down to eat.

Now, as he moved forward, he could see that what he had mistaken for shadows were the openings of other tunnels. Moving towards the first of these openings, he identified the noise as the slow plop of falling water. The same blue light gleamed in a ghostly way down the length of the passage. It was enough to show Alex the dank walls and the waterlogged floor. The tunnel was obviously unused. No one had walked down it recently as far as Alex could see. He dismissed it and moved on to the next one.

The next tunnel was dark. Alex racked his brains as to the source of the blue light. He was sure that somewhere in his training he would have learnt what caused this phenomenon. Whatever it was, the tunnel he faced now was unaffected by it. The blue light from the cavern lit the rim of the entrance but beyond that it stretched away into murky darkness.

Alex drew back from the mouth of the tunnel to search in his backpack for his flashlight which, though pencil-slim, had a powerful beam. He shone the light tentatively into the darkness. The beam, playing on the walls, ceiling and floor of the tunnel, showed only rock similar to that in the main cavern. He had no reason to suppose that beyond the reach of the flashlight's beam there was anything different. He was not here to explore tunnels, anyway. The mystery of the stopping-place which totally lacked any amenities was not his to solve. He could not afford to waste still more time.

He turned to leave, then with a sigh turned back. He could ignore the second tunnel with its blanket of darkness quite happily, but there was yet a third one. The thought of the earlier entrance, which he had not even glanced at, niggled at him. In failing to examine it he might have missed something vital to the race. He walked past the dank, unwelcoming opening of the first tunnel, past the gaping, black mouth of the second, towards the unknown aperture of the third.

Before he reached it, suddenly his head exploded with pain. A blackness, as dark as the impenetrable depths of the second tunnel, flooded over him, and he felt himself spiralling downwards on nerve-ends of pain into a complete darkness where he could feel nothing more.

Chapter five

When Alex surfaced from the depths of oblivion, his first thought was that somebody was torturing him. He had the vague feeling that all this had happened before. One moment there was red-hot pain and the next, biting cold. He moaned and tried to slip back into the merciful oblivion of unconsciousness. But someone was calling him and he felt a touch on his arm.

'Alex! Come on, Alex,' the voice said. He opened his eyes cautiously. Blue lights danced before him and the blurred outline of a face came into view. 'Come on, Alex. Easy does it.' Things were beginning to come into focus but the pain was still there.

'I feel sick,' Alex mumbled. The vomiting was worse than the pain, and he felt as if he was dying. It left him weak and trembling. But then he began to feel better and took the drink offered to him thankfully. He looked up to see Ricky smiling at him.

'Now you're beginning to look better,' Ricky said, handing him two medi-capsules. 'Take these. They'll clear your head completely.'

Alex put his hand tentatively to his head. 'Ouch,' he said. 'What happened?'

'Just what I was going to ask you.' Ricky eyed him quizzically.

Alex swallowed the capsules, then he turned his head carefully until he could look at the tunnel mouths.

'I was looking at the tunnels.' He tried hard to remember. 'I was going to look at that one over there, the third tunnel along, but . . .' He strained at the memory but it eluded him. His head throbbed. 'I can't remember. I suppose I must have stepped backwards and banged my head.' Everything was so confused. There were so many things that did not make sense. He couldn't think straight. 'Ricky, what are you doing here, anyway?' he asked.

Ricky turned away from him. Alex had not heard the approaching footsteps. Now he looked up to see Jeff walking towards them. 'Oh, good. You're OK now,' exclaimed Jeff, sounding pleased, as he drew nearer.

So Jeff was here too! Alex gave up trying to reason things out. He rubbed his head and attempted a grin. 'I suppose I'm feeling better. But what are you both doing here? Are you an emergency medic team or what?'

They both laughed. 'We're not the only ones here,' Jeff went on to explain. 'Seth's here too.'

'But this is crazy,' protested Alex, attempting to sit up, then deciding to make it a more cautious process. 'Why are we all here? I thought the idea of the computer test was to give a lead to those who were best at it and the endurance test too. I thought we were all heading in different directions to our spaceships.'

'Well, either three out of four people are wrong – or even three out of four computers! – or there's some crazy reasoning behind this that we've got to work out,' hazarded Ricky, adding as an afterthought, 'Of course, it could be a joke – testing our sense of humour. In which case you two might as well give up right now!'

Alex smiled and Jeff allowed the corners of his mouth to lift slightly. 'If you're feeling OK to move, Alex,' Jeff said, 'I don't think we should hang around here much longer than we have to.'

Ricky helped Alex slowly to his feet. The cave spun round, then steadied. 'OK,' said Alex. 'Let's go. But which way?'

'This way,' said Ricky, walking across to a tunnel in a part of the cavern Alex had not yet examined. 'I was exploring part of this system before you came. It's incredible. Just follow me.'

Ricky led them through a complex of tunnels and caves, dipping further down towards the centre of the planet as they went. Alex was already feeling light-headed as he walked along. Now he began to feel almost as if he were in a dream.

The caves were breathtaking. Always lit by the same blue light, sometimes shaded towards green, sometimes the colour of the summer sky, sometimes almost white, the caves were magical, each with a different spell of its own. Stalactites and stalagmites, pools and small water-falls combined with the strange shapes of rocks to make scenes which made Alex catch his breath in amazement. He completely forgot everything but the beauty of his surroundings.

The medi-capsules Ricky had given him had taken effect. Considering the injuries he had suffered since leaving the space shuttle, he was not feeling remarkably fit. The doubts and anxieties he had been experiencing lifted too in this atmosphere of peace and beauty, despite the fact that nothing had been resolved and the mystery had intensified since he had met with Ricky and Jeff.

He started in surprise when Jeff stopped suddenly

and put a finger to his lips, motioning to his two companions to be quiet. In the silence they heard the faint sound of soft movements in the cave they were about to enter. Jeff stole quietly into the cave while Alex and Ricky waited at the tunnel entrance. He stood perfectly still for a moment, studying whatever it was that was inside, before he turned and gestured to them to enter.

Walking cautiously into the cave, Alex was relieved to see that there was nothing to fear. It was a high-ceilinged, shadowy place. The rocks on one side climbed like a giant staircase into the hidden darkness. In the centre was a pool, faintly luminous in the soft silver-blue light. Crouched at the edge of the pool was Seth.

They had not made any noise as they entered the cave. However, at their arrival, Seth turned quickly. In that brief moment, before he had himself under control, Alex glimpsed a fleeting expression on Seth's bullish face that could have been fear or guilt. As Seth rose hastily, his face set once more into a sullen scowl, Alex caught the swift movement of a small object flying through the air to land in the pool at the centre of the cave.

'What was that you just threw away, Seth?' demanded Jeff quietly.

'What business is it of yours what I do, Mr Super-Brain?' snarled Seth. 'I didn't throw anything away anyway!'

'Hey, isn't it great having a reunion like this!' joked Ricky. 'Hi, Seth. D'you come here often?'

'I see wonder boy has joined us,' sneered Seth, ignoring Ricky and glaring at Alex. 'Thought you'd have been planting your little flag on top of old Anderloss by now, Alex.'

Alex bit back a sharp retort and, ignoring Seth, turned to Ricky. 'Let's move out of here and get on with this race, shall we?'

'No. Wait a minute,' interrupted Jeff. 'Did either of you see something land in the pool as we came in? I was watching you, Seth, and whatever you were taking just now wasn't part of your provisions. How do you manage all that extra drive and energy, Seth? Part of your training course, is it?'

Before Alex had time to move, Seth had jumped on Jeff, grabbing at his suit so that he pulled him off balance. His face was livid with rage as he blurted out his question. 'And just what are you trying to say?'

'I'm saying that if I had proof, I'd have you disqualified from this race,' replied Jeff coolly, shaking himself free with a neat movement.

'Well, we thought this race would have been finished by now,' came a familiar voice high up on the other side of the cave. All four of them turned to look as Ben and Callie stepped nimbly down from the rocks to join them. 'This is a nice surprise,' smiled Ben.

'Whatever are you all doing here?' asked Callie, looking perplexed.

Alex looked at Ben with mingled surprise and relief. He could not help shifting his eyes to Ben's legs. For the first time it occurred to him that Ben's call for help could have been a trick. Could it have been Ben who had made the first call that had lured him to the dragon rock and then, when his trick had failed, tried an SOS call of a different kind? Ben's mild manner could be just a front. He certainly didn't look like someone whose leg had been caught in a trap.

'Thought you two were going to be alone, did you?' asked Ricky, arching his eyebrows and giving Callie a knowing wink.

Callie turned from him indignantly. 'Alex, what are we all doing here?' she asked.

Alex shrugged his shoulders. Ricky voiced the answer for him. 'Your guess is as good as ours! Maybe testing us with little surprises is their idea of a fun-filled race!'

'What were you saying about Seth being disqualified from the race?' asked Ben, turning to Jeff.

Seth looked about to explode again. Alex felt he'd had about enough. There seemed to be some competitors who had no right to be in the race at all! He looked Ben squarely in the eye. 'Maybe Jeff's suggesting that some people in this race wouldn't be above cheating.' He deliberately let his gaze drop to Ben's legs.

Ben looked at him steadily, but it was Callie who spoke. 'If you're wondering about Ben's leg, Alex, it's pretty badly bruised, and it's no thanks to you that it's not broken. When Ben couldn't get help from the first person he contacted, he called me. It was only because I've done a special course in laser and soft ray treatment that I was able to get his leg free.' She paused to fix Alex with a cool look. 'And it's only because my training unit sent me on an advanced first aid course that Ben is walking now. I think you owe him an apology, Alex, don't you?'

There was a brief embarrassed silence before Ben spoke quietly. 'I think Callie was obviously the right one to answer my SOS. I think what we should be asking though is this – If the Waste Zone is uninhabited, who set that trap?'

It was a dramatic moment. No one spoke as the implications of the question sank home.

Alex, still reeling from Callie's accusation, felt his initial sense of guilt and shame replaced by a sudden churning of his stomach, and a feeling of unease at hearing the question he had been asking himself, voiced by someone else. But now there was a new dimension to the problem. Alex had assumed that if there was someone behind the incidents it was another competitor. Ben's observation put things in a new, disturbing light. Either one of them was resorting to some pretty low tricks to win the race, or the Waste Zone was not uninhabited after all.

In that moment of silence they all became aware of something strange happening in the cave. It was only as they began to feel hot that they realised that the temperature in the cave had been pleasantly warm since they had entered. Now the heat increased rapidly, and Alex rubbed droplets of sweat from his eyes. The colour of the pool was changing, like light caught in a prism. They watched, fascinated, as the waters of the pool danced through a spectrum of colour until it became deep flame. Seconds before the hissing noise began, Jeff was the first one to come to his senses. He grabbed Callie and pulled her back to the shelter of the rocks, yelling to the others, 'Stand back! Quick! Get down!'

Suddenly the waters gathered and gushed into a huge fountain of glowing red. Alex felt the panic rising in his mind as the waters of the pool rose with a deafening roar. Above the noise of the waters he heard Jeff yell, 'Run, all of you! Run!'

Chapter six

For a second they all stood frozen, their eyes fixed in horror and fascination on the fountain of boiling water. In moments the air became thick with fumes that filled their nostrils and made them choke. Jeff's warning shouts were cut off by a spasm of coughing. He pulled the collar of his jacket across the lower half of his face and launched himself into action. Lunging across the cave, he pulled Callie with him, dragging her out. After that things happened quickly. Alex had no idea afterwards how they all got out of the cave. He himself stumbled blindly, his eyes stinging so that he could not see, and his mouth and nose filled with the acrid smoke which made it hard to breathe.

Out in the tunnel, when clear air told them they were free from the toxic effects of the fountain of flame, they all slumped against the walls, thirstily drinking in gulps of pure, fresh air. Alex dropped down onto the tunnel floor and, leaning backwards, closed his eyes.

'Where's Seth? Seth's not here!'

Callie's anxious voice brought his eyes flying open. Ricky was sitting with his back against the wall. Ben was crouched down with his head in his hands. Jeff, looking white, was standing sideways to the wall. Callie was sitting in the middle of the tunnel floor, looking anxiously around. Seth was nowhere to be seen.

'The cave!' exclaimed Ben springing to his feet. 'He's still in the cave!'

'I'll go.' Jeff laid a firm hand on Ben's shoulders, stopping him, and moved off quickly back towards the cave.

Ben began stumblingly to follow him until Callie's sharp cry halted him in his tracks.

'Ben! No! Let Jeff go. He knows what he's doing. If he's not back in a couple of minutes then someone else can go in.'

Alex was beginning to wonder if the time had come to put Callie's suggestion into action when they heard the sounds of Jeff's return. First came the noise of coughing, then dragging footsteps. Alex moved to his feet as Ben rushed forward. They met Jeff a little way down the tunnel. He was supporting a stunned Seth who coughed and groaned as he leaned heavily on Jeff.

As Ben moved forward to help him with his burden, Jeff told them how he had found Seth near the entrance of the cave. The fountain was subsiding and the air, though still filled with smoke, was not so dense. All the same, it had been a near thing that Jeff had got Seth out of the cave before his lungs had filled with toxic fumes.

While Jeff was talking, Callie sat Seth quietly down. He sat dazed with his head in his hands. When Callie offered him a drink he took the beaker eagerly and drank greedily.

'What was that back in the cave?' asked Ben quietly. 'This is the strangest place. Do you think that fountain was part of the test? A kind of obstacle in the race?'

Jeff, who had been sitting with his eyes closed, looked up at Ben. 'No,' he said firmly. 'I don't think that what happened in the cave had anything to do with the race.' His voice dropped and a worried expression crossed his face. 'At least I don't think it was anything that Captain Rudge or the organizers planned.'

Alex stared at Jeff wide-eyed. If Jeff meant what Alex thought he meant, that someone was sabotaging the race, then it seemed the tricks were not over. In fact, this latest episode with the pool and the fire could have proved more dangerous than anything that had gone before.

'Oh, come on, Jeff.' Ricky's voice, tinged with sarcasm, bit into Alex's thoughts. 'Get real. You're not suggesting that fire was a set-up? There's probably a perfectly reasonable explanation.'

'Like what?' asked Jeff.

'A fire-breathing water dragon,' suggested Ricky, pulling what was intended to be a funny face.

'Of course,' returned Jeff. 'Why didn't I think of that?'

Ricky's humour was, as usual, no help. Alex felt a gnawing fear. If there really was someone playing tricks, there were probably worse things to come. The thought niggled at him that he ought to voice his fears. Ben had said what he thought earlier and now Jeff was airing his suspicions. Should Alex share the strange things that had happened to him? Would the others take him seriously if he did? Sooner or later someone could suffer really badly from one of these supposed accidents. Alex would wish then that he had spoken now. He cleared his throat, but before he could speak everyone's attention was drawn to Seth.

'No. No!' Seth lifted glazed eyes to look at Callie without seeing her. 'I didn't do it,' he said hoarsely. 'But I do have to win, I have to win the race.'

Callie looked worriedly from Jeff to Ben. 'He's suffering from shock. I think we ought to get him back to Base.'

Jeff nodded. 'If we can get him to my spaceship I'll take him.' Then, as a thought occurred to him, he added, 'No. On second thoughts, if you all stay with him here, I'll fetch my ship. He doesn't look fit to be moved.'

Alex wondered if Jeff was in any fit state himself to go wandering off across the treacherous Waste Zone. But there was a quiet authority and determination about him that kept Alex from protesting.

The atmosphere after Jeff had gone was strained. Suddenly, after hours of putting themselves under pressure to make fast progress, they were all left with nothing to do but wait.

'Will it be fair to Jeff if we carry on the race without him once he's taken Seth back to Base?' asked Ben tentatively, breaking the silence.

Or fair to Seth, Alex wondered. He had felt sorry for Seth at the desperation in his voice when he had moaned about needing to win.

'Perhaps the question you should be asking,' said Ricky, for once completely serious, 'is this – "is Jeff being fair to us?" How do we know that, when he gets to his spaceship, he'll fly it back here? How do we know he won't go straight to Anderloss? He'll have no competition at all if he climbs the mountain and plants his flag.'

There was a moment's horrified silence, then Callie said slowly, 'No. No, I don't think so. Jeff risked getting hurt when he went back into the cave for Seth. I don't think that was an act.'

'Just because people do some good things, doesn't mean they're not capable of doing bad things as well,' argued Ricky.

'If Jeff does do that — which I don't think he will,' interposed Ben, 'we can get him disqualified. I think we've no choice but to wait. It would be sensible though to move Seth as near to the exit from the caves as possible so he'll be ready for Jeff to collect.'

'Come on, Seth, on your feet,' Ben coaxed.

Seth's only response was a groan. However, he allowed Ben and Alex to lever him to his feet and lead him down the tunnel to another cave. He managed the journey without protest, but at the entrance to the small cave he swayed.

'I don't feel too good,' he muttered, putting an unsteady hand to his head.

It was Alex's opinion that he didn't look too good either. His face had a sickly tinge of grey. But his eyes, although narrowed in pain, were clear again. Callie, to Alex's surprise, seemed pleased with Seth.

'Looks like the effect of the fumes is wearing off,' she whispered to Alex. She approached Seth, smiling reassuringly. 'Seth, I'm going to give you a couple of capsules. They'll help stop any nausea or dizziness you may feel.'

'I don't feel dizzy or sick,' protested Seth gruffly and sank down onto the floor of the cave.

Callie crouched down beside him, offering the capsules. 'Take these anyway,' she insisted.

'What's the matter with me?' asked Seth pitifully.

'A question it would take too long to answer right now,' quipped Ricky.

'You'll feel OK in a minute or two,' said Callie encouragingly, giving Ricky a frosty glance. 'I don't think he needs to be taken back to Base, do you?' she added with an enquiring look at Ben and Alex. 'I know he doesn't look too good, but he is improving rapidly. I think by the time Jeff gets back Seth should be almost up to carrying on with race.'

'*If* Jeff gets back,' said Ricky darkly. 'I think if he's not back in half an hour from now, we should carry on with the race anyway.'

Alex looked uncertainly from Ben to Callie. It could be Jeff who was sabotaging the race. If that was so, then they shouldn't let him delay them by keeping them waiting in the caverns.

'I think Jeff will be back,' Ben said firmly. Alex looked at him in surprise. This Ben seemed a very different person from the hesitant boy who had started the race. 'But,' he continued, 'if he isn't back in half an hour, let's decide then what we should do. In the meantime, if you think we can manage it, Callie, we'll have another go at making our way to the exit of the caverns.'

'Walking should actually help him now,' commented Callie. 'Come on, Seth,' she coaxed, 'back on your feet.'

Supported by Ben and Callie, Seth managed to make steady progress along the tunnel. His progress was too slow for Ricky, it seemed. He strode off ahead of the others. Alex watched him with some misgivings until a bend in the tunnel took him out of sight. There was no sign of him when they negotiated the bend, but the entrance of the next cave was now in sight.

The cave was perhaps the largest they had entered. Alex caught his breath at the awesome sight before him. The tunnel floor, which had brought them to the cave, divided just a little way inside the entrance to form two high ledges which hugged the cave walls. In the centre the floor dropped away to form a wide basin some thirty feet below. Above their heads the roof rose into a lofty, cathedral-like vault. Directly ahead the two wings of the ledge joined again before the entrance to another tunnel. There was no sign of Ricky. The cave was empty.

Callie and Ben, with Seth between them, had begun to move cautiously along the ledge to their right. About half-way round the cave they stopped suddenly, and Callie gave a gasp of alarm. Alex moved as quickly as he could towards them, expecting that perhaps the ledge at their feet was crumbling away. Callie's gaze, however, was not on the ground but was fixed on the tunnel entrance at the far side.

Following her gaze, Alex saw with a shock that the cave was not empty after all. There were two figures standing there, one on either side of the entrance. They almost blended in with the stone behind them. The squat creatures would probably reach no higher than Alex's shoulder, but it was not their size that was daunting. Low foreheads and bushy eyebrows protruded over faces that were almost dark grey. Their stocky bodies bulged with powerful muscles. The total effect was one of menace held barely in check.

They had appeared so silently it was hard to believe they were real. Alex wished that they were not. The only comforting thought was that there were only two of them. Alex and the others could at least retreat the way they had come. It was only as he looked back that Alex saw two more figures, each armed with a shaft of shining silver.

Chapter seven

Alex gulped. He blinked to see if he was hallucinating. This was incredible. The race for which he had trained, and to which he had looked forward for so long, was turning into a nightmare. In a way he felt numb, as if he had passed beyond fear. 'Hi, boys,' he said.

'Careful,' whispered Ben in his ear. 'I've read up on Rock Men. They can be pretty hostile.'

'But Rock Men don't exist,' protested Callie. 'They're only a legend.'

'You tell them that,' said Ben.

The Rock Men stood silently watching them.

'What do they want?' whispered Callie.

'They're waiting for someone,' replied Ben. 'They just seem to want to keep us here.'

'I'm not staying,' Seth blurted out. His voice was tight with fear and his face was flushed. It seemed he was almost back to normal at exactly the wrong moment, Alex thought with a pang of alarm, and as if he might try something rash like rushing at the two armed Rock Men.

'You're right. None of us is staying,' said Ben quietly. 'I've got a plan.'

To Alex's relief Seth calmed down and gave his full attention to Ben.

Alex was glad that Ben knew so much about the legend of the Rock Men. They believed in magic – spirits of the rocks and water and trees. Even in the highly technological society of today, Rock Men held on to primitive beliefs as old as the planet itself. Callie's assumption that Rock Men didn't exist was fairly commonplace, Ben explained. Rock Men lived only in some of the undeveloped mountainous regions and even there they kept themselves hidden. What was strange, commented Ben, was not that Rock Men existed but that they were allowing themselves to be seen.

'They look pretty fierce,' he finished in a low voice, 'but I'd bet they're more afraid of us than we are of them. If we can startle them, we may catch them off guard. The problem is we mustn't panic them into using those unfriendly-looking spears. If my guess is right they don't intend using those spears, but if they get panicky they might. What we're going to do is entertain them with a little firework display!'

In their packs each of them carried a bundle of special effect explosives which could be used in emergencies in a variety of ways – to signal for help, as a source of heat or light, or to blast through a thin layer of rock. Four bundles combined and dropped into the central basin of the cave would cause quite an effect.

It was a good idea. Alex was impressed. He was even more impressed when Ben began a steady flow of speech in a strange tongue which set the Rock Men looking at each other nervously. While Ben talked, Alex and Callie carefully assembled the package of explosives. Later Ben explained that he had told the Rock Men the spirits of the cave were angry and, unless the four travellers were allowed to leave, they would show their anger. At the time the only words Alex understood were those Ben slipped in to give the signal for action. 'Ready when you are. Let's go for it!'

For the first time one of their plans went smoothly and without a single hitch. The explosives shot up like fireworks in a dazzling array of colours and golden rain, then they emitted a thick screen of green smoke, behind which the four companions were able to make their way to the tunnel entrance through which Ricky must have gone earlier. They took the guards by surprise. Ben knocked one out and Alex, coming up behind him, dealt with the other. To their relief there were no more guards in the tunnel and, to their surprise and delight, the tunnel led out into the open air.

For a moment they stood stunned, unable to believe they had not walked into yet another trap. They waited, carefully looking around them. It seemed the Rock Men were not coming out after them. They were free at last to carry on with the race.

But there was the problem of having to wait for Jeff. They argued briefly about what they should do. Ben was for delaying the race until Jeff got back. Callie thought they should only wait for another half an hour. If Jeff was not back by that time, she argued, he was not coming back.

Alex thought of Ricky forging ahead. He didn't want to waste another second waiting. But he said nothing. The others were right. They should wait for Jeff, but not indefinitely. They might wait for ever if Jeff was the one who was sabotaging the race.

Seth had hunched down on the sandy ground, leaning back against the rock face. He had managed the dash from the cave unaided, but the effort had tired him – though not as much as Alex had expected. Without looking up, he spoke gruffly. 'If you're so worried about

Jeff, why don't you call him on the radio? Or is that too simple and straightforward for a bunch of geniuses like you?'

There was a moment's silence as Seth's words hit home. Alex could have kicked himself. He should have thought of using the radio after his recent experiences. Seth was right. They were all trying to be so clever they were being stupid. He glanced embarrassed, at Callie and Ben, and was puzzled to catch a gleam in Ben's eye. Even as Alex watched him, Ben's face broke into a smile then crumpled into helpless laughter. Seth looked up, taken aback. This was not the effect he had expected his words to have.

Callie, without knowing why, was smiling too. 'Come on, Ben. Share the joke.'

Ben managed to control himself enough to say, 'In my Practical Intelligence test I scored 93.'

Alex felt his mouth gape. He had never heard of anyone scoring over 80. And this was the boy he had thought was stupid!

'Intelligence: 93,' Ben continued, still laughing. 'Common Sense: nil! You're right, Seth. If I'm anything to go by, I think the SESU will collapse when the winner of this race joins it! Alex, I think you'd better contact Jeff.'

Alex grimaced. His track record making radio contact in the race so far also merited nil.

Callie, without any idea she was touching a raw nerve, added jokingly, 'Think you can manage that without any help, Alex?'

'I wouldn't bet on it,' Alex returned and, pressing the necessary buttons, he tried to make contact with Jeff.

Jeff's voice came back almost immediately. It was loud and clear. Alex could even hear the hint of anxiety as Jeff asked, 'Is everything OK? Seth still all right?'

Alex explained that it was because Seth was so much better that they were calling. There was no need for Jeff to run him back to Base.

'I'll come back anyway.' Jeff sounded doubtful. He obviously could not imagine the Seth he had dragged out of the cave being fit enough to carry on.

Alex was still groping for the words to put Jeff's mind at ease when Seth pushed rudely against him and yelled into the microphone. 'Jeff, this is Seth. I'm fine. Come back for me if you like, but if you do it'll be a wasted journey. I won't be here. I'll see you on top of Anderloss – or back at Base!'

If Seth had wanted to create a stir then he had succeeded. Jeff's voice, taken aback, questioning, came over the radio, but it was a minute or two before Alex answered, for he, like Ben and Callie, could only stare at Seth in disbelief. Seth now looked so completely himself that if Alex had not seen the condition he was in earlier he would not have believed Seth had been so ill.

Ben was the first to find his voice. 'Seth, you can't just go off to Anderloss.' As his words tailed off Alex thought he had been going to add 'in the state you're in', but Seth now looked as fit as any of them.

'Can't I?' Seth replied with a smirk. 'Watch me!' He turned on his heels and, looking down at his compass reading, walked off.

'Seth! Wait!' called Callie. 'I'll come with you.'

Seth did not even falter. He obviously had no intention of waiting for anyone.

'No,' said Ben sharply, grasping Callie's arm to stop her. 'Let him go.'

Alex had been watching the unexpected drama

enacted before him in an almost hypnotic state. Jeff's anxious voice on the radio finally penetrated his numbed brain. 'Alex?' Jeff was asking. 'Alex, are you there? What's happening?'

It took a matter of minutes to put Jeff in the picture and to make new arrangements. Jeff suggested that the three of them set out immediately in search of their spaceships before Seth had too much of a start. He himself would return to the spot where he had picked up his ship and wait until he had cancelled out the time advantage he had gained. Then he would set out for Anderloss.

As Alex conferred with Ben and Callie, it struck him that the race which had once seemed the most important thing in the world, did not seem so important now. The thought of competing against Ben and Callie seemed almost alien to him. They had become close, like members of a team.

The thought of getting ahead of Seth was quite appealing, but beating him presented no real challenge when he had played so unfairly. Overtaking Ricky would take some doing though, as he had an impossibly long head start. Besides, the same thing applied. Where would be the sense of achievement in beating Ricky, who had cheated, leaving the others in the caves before Seth had recovered, while he forged on ahead alone?

Thinking of cheating, Alex recalled something else about Seth. Hadn't someone accused him of throwing something into the pool in the cave where the fire had erupted? The implication was that Seth had taken something, perhaps a drug of some kind, to ensure that he was the fittest and fastest to win the race.

Who was it who had made that accusation? Alex could not remember. Was someone unmasking Seth's dishonesty, or was someone throwing the scent off their own trail by diverting suspicion? The fact that Seth had headed off on his own now, without waiting for them to reach an agreement with Jeff, did not argue well for him. On the other hand, he had said what he thought. He saw no reason to stay. Alex had to admit he simply did not know what to think.

Alex forced his thoughts back to the present to find Ben and Callie deep in conversation. He had just been wondering if he should share his qualms about Ricky and Seth with them. Now he hesitated. Ben and Callie, both so meek and helpful, seemed to have stayed well in the background of this race. Ben and Callie, who had arrived at the caves together . . .

A part of Alex hated himself for his suspicions. Another part reminded him that he had heard strange voices on the radio. Someone was trying to stop him running this race. He had no evidence yet whether it was one of the other competitors or someone else. He would be a fool not to be cautious. He must be wary of everyone.

Ben and Callie, it appeared, had been checking their compass readings. They waited now for Alex to check his. It was as they had expected. Their directions differed. They agreed to follow their separate paths without any further communication until the end of the race. Each of them was still to attempt to get to Anderloss first.

Alex's course now took him across country away from the rock face. Callie disappeared in an eastward direction, while Ben continued to follow the line of the cliff. Alex did not envy him. He was not sorry to leave a place where fiery fountains bubbled up from pools and

Rock Men appeared from nowhere, armed with sharp silver spears.

Despite all that had happened, Alex began to feel the excitement of the race once more as he pressed on alone. The terrain was now familiar and the last lap of the journey was short and uneventful. He reached the location of his compass reading fairly quickly. It was a sheltered basin with jagged rocks edging its rim. He was relieved to see that his spaceship stood there as planned, a neat, compact oval disc, its matt surface of steel and chrome blending in with the grey landscape.

The thought came to him, unbidden, that maybe things were too easy. What if a trap lay ahead? Alex almost envied his father his optimistic, easy-going outlook on life. On the other hand, Alex had proved that you could manage to survive dangers and cope with all kinds of crises without leaning on the crutch of believing that a God, who didn't exist anyway, would scurry round, rescuing you from trouble. He did not like the extremely suspicious turn of mind his thoughts seemed always to be taking. But it was not without cause. Perhaps, in the course of the race so far, he had not been cautious enough.

He pressed the electronic device to activate the mechanism which opened the spaceship door and let down a narrow, metal ladder for him to climb aboard. At the top of the steps, Alex looked carefully round the small cockpit and storage area. He felt a thrill of pride as he noted the plushly carpeted floors and walls, the supple leather seats for the pilot and co-pilot in a matching shade of coffee brown. The gleam of the instrument panel and fittings showed that the ship was brand new. With one last glance round, Alex took his seat at the controls. Everything seemed in perfect order. He felt the familiar thrill as his ship soared into the air, then sped smoothly forward.

He had calculated that he was within minutes of sighting Anderloss when he heard a faint, unfamiliar noise. He hesitated a moment before turning, feeling reluctant to face any potential crisis now when everything was going so well. The second's hesitation brought disaster. There behind him, unbelievably, stood Seth, his laser gun pointed at Alex's back.

'Keep going,' he ordered Alex. 'Hope you don't mind me joining you. I thought, since you'd all been so worried about me, you would probably be quite pleased to give me a lift to Anderloss! There seems to be something wrong with my ship. Lucky for us both that yours was so close. Now we can share it and, when we arrive, you can have a nice rest while I pop out and plant the flag. My flag, of course, Alex.'

It was fortunate that Seth talked so much. It gave Alex the chance to judge the moment for catching him off guard. He threw himself at Seth, knocking his gun to the floor. If he had been thinking clearly he would not have risked leaving the controls. It would have been better to wait. As it was, he realised just too late that, if he didn't do something immediately, they would crash. Seth had him in a tight grip when suddenly the ship jolted and, with an uncomfortably loud droning noise, spiralled down through a tangle of trees and bushes to land with a crash at the foot of Anderloss Mountain.

Chapter eight

Gingerly Alex raised himself up into a sitting position. There was blood oozing from a gash in his left arm where he had caught it against the metal edge of the galley door. Apart from that, he found to his surprise that he was unhurt. As Seth had suddenly released his grip, Alex had staggered backwards to fall against the carpeted wall and then, with the roll of the ship, had slumped to the floor. Seth had fallen in the opposite direction. Now he lay sprawled on his back against the far wall of the cockpit.

The cockpit swam out of focus and steadied again. Seth, Alex saw hazily, was trying to lever himself up. 'You stupid fool,' Seth began, his eyes narrowed in a scornful glare. Then, even as Alex watched with a mixture of anger at Seth's words and relief that he was all right, Seth fainted.

Alex gaped for a moment in dismay, then he slowly attempted to get to his feet. The movement, careful as it was, started his arm throbbing with such an intensity of pain that Alex hardly knew what to do with himself. He gulped down a double dose of medi-capsules and sat quietly for a few moments, fighting nausea and dizziness. When he was sure he could move without being sick or fainting, he crossed over to Seth.

It didn't look to him as if Seth was badly injured in any way. He hadn't sounded as if he was hurt. The impact of the crash had been softened by the mesh of trees and bushes through which the ship had fallen. Alex thought he and Seth had been very lucky. But the jolting of the rough landing and delayed shock, on top of everything else he had gone through, had probably been too much for Seth, so he had passed out. Alex was rather relieved that he had.

Just in case he came round unexpectedly, Alex picked up Seth's laser gun and took it with him as he made his way slowly to the small galley behind the cockpit. He put the gun down on a work surface, then searched in the medicare cabinet for ointment and a bandage to dress his arm. Trying to fix the bandage single-handed was a frustrating and exhausting task. Eventually it was done and Alex bathed his face, hot with perspiration, in the cool water at the small hand basin. He realised belatedly that this utility area was a part of his ship he had not checked. Seth must have sneaked in while he was examining the controls.

Knowing what to do about Seth was a problem. When Alex turned back into the main cabin he was relieved to see that Seth had not moved. He checked his pulse and found it to be steady. Seth's breathing was even, though he was obviously still out cold. Alex debated whether to radio back to Base to alert them to what had happened. Now that he was in his spaceship he could use his radio. Strictly it was against the rules, but surely it was the right course of action in an emergency such as this.

Except that the radio did not work.

This left Alex with an agonizing decision. Should he stay with Seth until he came to, or could he safely leave him and continue the race? He felt rather annoyed. They had helped Seth when he could not have managed on his own, and look at the thanks they got. Seth did not deserve any sacrifice on Alex's part.

He smiled ruefully. Perhaps his father's ideas had got hold of him despite himself. The idea of looking after somebody else, even if they didn't deserve it, was one that applied in this case. Alex could not really leave Seth in the state he was in. For a fleeting moment he envied his father. In a situation like this Alex's father would be able to ask his God what he should do. Even when the thing that needed to be done wasn't easy, at least there was the comfort of knowing you were doing the right thing. However, it was a comfort that Alex would have to do without. All he could rely on was his own judgment. It seemed to him he had no choice but to stay.

Meanwhile he and Seth still needed to be rescued. He didn't want to delay any of the others if someone was about to win the race. But he needed someone to help him with Seth and to ferry him back to Base if necessary. The radio on his wrist console would have helped, but he had noticed while bandaging his arm that the console was damaged.

What, then, was Alex to do? Waiting here till the others got back to Base, and someone noticed that he and Seth were missing, was going to take hours. He could of course try to bring Seth round. Perhaps that was what he ought to do. But from his recent experience of Seth's behaviour that might not be a good idea. It would be too much like waking a hungry wild animal that would be only too pleased to find its next meal sitting in front of it. Right or not, Alex felt that he had enough to cope with without inviting more trouble from

Seth. He needed help.

Alex's heart lifted as he realised that there was really only one course open to him. He would have to go and look for help. He must find Callie or Ben or Jeff – perhaps even Ricky. There was only one place where Alex could expect to find any – perhaps all – of them for, although their compass readings had taken them in different directions, they would all converge on Anderloss Mountain. Alex might as well make his way to the top of Anderloss too. It was actually the best course of action, after all, for him to complete the race.

Making one last check on Seth, and a double check on the engine and electrical circuits to make sure there was no danger of a fire or explosion while he was gone, Alex made his way cautiously out of the ship.

As he reached the door and pushed it open, Alex appreciated for the first time the angle at which the ship had landed. With the ship sloping to the left-hand side, the door swung open easily enough. It would have been a different matter altogether if the ship had crashed tilting in the other direction. It also meant that it was not too long a drop to the ground. Alex took a deep breath and jumped.

The landing was not all that he would have hoped for. The breath was knocked out of him, every bone in his body was jarred and, as his feet hit the damp ground, his left foot slipped and he fell awkwardly onto his right side. The only good thing about it was that it was not the side of his injured arm.

For a moment he lay still, noting every ache and pain objectively, as if they belonged to someone else. Then he began to shiver as the cold air, sweeping down the slopes of Anderloss, bit through his protective clothing. The cold forced him to his feet.

He was able to stand. He still felt curiously detached from what was happening to him. It was a strange feeling. The fact that he could stand meant that he had not sprained, twisted or broken his ankle when he slipped. He supposed this was a good thing. It meant that he could carry on, forcing his frozen, aching limbs to move towards the icy, towering slopes of the snow-clad, craggy mountain that was Anderloss.

If he'd had a spaceship that was in working order, he thought, he would have given up there and then. He would have climbed into the warm cockpit, lowered his aching limbs into the seat behind the controls, and let the ship take him back to Base and civilization. No one in their right minds would put raw cadets through the ordeal of a race like this. The training had been totally inadequate for the trials he had faced. He seemed to have spent most of the past few hours suffering in one way or another. He did not know why, but the awkward landing as he jumped hopefully from the spaceship had somehow been the last straw.

While Alex's mind retreated into a cosy fantasy of withdrawing from the race, his plodding footsteps took him nearer and nearer to Anderloss. He walked, without really noticing, from the damp ground in which a bedraggled carpet of weedy grass struggled to survive, on to a crisp, silvery expanse of glistening snow which began at the base of the mountain, rising to cover Anderloss like icing on a gigantic, grey, rugged cake.

If Alex had been concentrating, if his mind had been fully alert, he might have avoided what happened next, though it happened completely without warning. He stepped forward only to feel the soft snow giving way beneath him. It was so quick and so unexpected that he could do nothing about it. The snow, which had reached only Alex's ankles, was suddenly up to his waist.

In that split second of sinking, a cold wave of fear cleared Alex's mind. He knew more than anything else that he wanted to climb Anderloss. Despite everything, he still wanted desperately to win the race. He did not want to lose his life here in this snowdrift. But, now that he knew clearly and certainly what he wanted to do, now that the urge to try his best had returned, he was helpless. He was completely powerless to save himself.

His flailing arms sank in the soft snow. There was no handhold for his frantic, grasping fingers. There was no one around to help him. Desperately he shouted for help. His muffled voice floated uselessly away into silence. The effort of shouting, however, disturbed the drift and he sank deeper, up to his chest, in the engulfing snow.

Chapter nine

Alex now knew that in all the ordeals he had faced over the past few hours, in all the frightening experiences he had been through in his entire life, he had never before known real fear. He felt as if he had stepped out over the edge of a pit, unable to stop himself from falling into a vast emptiness which filled him with terror. He was like a trapped animal facing the hunter, knowing with dread that this time there would be no escape. It was only a matter of time before he was swallowed up in the snow at the foot of Anderloss itself.

But one small part of his mind refused to give up hope. Surely there must be something he could do. He hardly dared move. In a short time he would not be able to move anyway, numbed by the bitter cold. All he had left was that small part of his mind which was not frozen with fear. He forced himself to try and think clearly. Perhaps, somewhere in the training he had recently undergone, there was something he could remember? No. He was sure there was not. He felt despair closing in on him like a fog, blotting out the sight of everything normal and familiar.

Then the picture came suddenly, surprising him in its startling clarity. It was almost as if he were there. It was two summers ago that he and his father had climbed, on a blue-skied day, into the mountains behind their home. There was a lake nestling in a pocket of hills against a backdrop of lush, feathery trees. They had spent the afternoon fishing. Most of the time they had sat in silence by the lake-side, drinking in the peace and basking in the warmth of the lovely summer day. But they had also talked. It had been that kind of special time when you could share thoughts and dreams that you would not normally talk about. At the time Alex had not paid too much attention to what his father had said. In fact he was surprised that he remembered it. Now, however, his father's words came back clearly.

'Alex, I know this won't mean much to you now. You have your whole life ahead of you, exciting things to do, all kinds of fascinating experiences to enjoy; but I want you to think about this. God does exist, Alex. I know you don't believe that and I can't prove it to you. He may not seem real to you, but you are very real to him. He created you. He loves you, has great plans for you. I want you to remember that, Alex. If you are ever in trouble, even if you aren't sure whether he exists, he'll be there for you. Just talk to him. Ask him for help. OK, Alex?'

Alex must have protested. He couldn't remember. He had a clear picture though of his father, perched on a rock on the lake shore, looking at him with a smile in his green eyes. 'No. I'm not asking you to sort the universe out before you agree with what I've just said. Just remember, will you, Alex? Just remember.'

Alex could see his younger self sitting there in the sunshine, nodding his head. And he had remembered. For a fleeting moment the warmth of the sunlit afternoon washed over him, then he was back in the numbing cold of the snowdrift, facing death. Except that now he had something he could do. It didn't make much sense to him, but it was at least something.

How did you talk to someone you didn't think existed, he wondered. Well, if God didn't exist, it didn't matter what he said. Alex had nothing to lose.

'Look, God, I've always thought you didn't exist . . .' he began. Then he stopped. That didn't really make any sense. Perhaps there wasn't any need for a lot of words. Perhaps he needed only to say what was on his heart. 'Help me,' he said, forcing the words out between numb lips. His breath frosted on the air. 'Please. Please. I'm so frightened. I don't see how I can get out of this and I don't want to die. God, help me please.' His voice caught on the word 'please' and he felt tears start in his eyes. 'Please.' He framed the word silently with his lips, then he closed his eyes. A tear trickled down his cheek.

When he opened his eyes nothing had changed. Anderloss loomed above him, wreathed in snow, its slopes and summit bare. There was no one about and no sign or sound that anyone might be approaching. The cold continued to bite into him and he felt increasingly more numb. If there was any difference, it was perhaps that he had lost the only thing he had left, some semblance of dignity. There was no one to see, but he would have been ashamed if anyone had seen how he had pleaded with a God he didn't believe in, and how he had almost been reduced to tears. He felt almost hot with shame.

Thinking about how he felt made him realise, with a small sense of shock, that things had actually changed. The paralysing sense of fear was gone. He could not exactly say that he had a sense of peace about his predicament, but he certainly no longer felt afraid.

He also began to hope, for the first time, that he might survive. The soft sifting of the snow seemed for some unaccountable reason to have stopped. He was still bitterly cold and so tightly wedged in the snow that he could not pull himself out, but there no longer seemed any danger of him sinking further into the snowdrift.

Alex was still marvelling at this new state of affairs when another incredible thing happened. In the far distance, at the furthest extreme of the foot of Anderloss, he thought he saw a small, black speck moving against the blinding white of the snow.

Straining his eyes to keep the figure in sight, Alex lifted his stiffening arms. Even that small movement would have sent him sinking further into the snow if he had attempted it earlier. Now he was able slowly and painfully to bring his arms together so that he could rub them a little. He wanted to be able to wave his arm to attract attention when whoever it was came nearer. He tried a tentative call but his voice was too weak to carry far.

He winced at the fierce, tingling sensation as the feeling began to come back into his arms, then forgot the nagging pain completely as a wave of panic and disappointment washed over him. The speck, which had been coming nearer, had now disappeared completely from sight. Alex forced a cry from between cracked lips but he had no hope of it carrying so far. It seemed as if the unknown figure was going to climb the mountain from that far side. The feeling of despondency that swept over Alex was all the keener because he had believed, for a moment, that his rescue was only a matter of time.

Although his common sense told him that it was a waste of time, Alex kept his eyes trained steadily on the spot where he had seen the figure disappear. As time passed and there was no sign of movement of any kind, he told himself that keeping hope alive, when there was no longer any reason for hope, was only going to make things harder for him. Yet he could not tear his eyes away and kept up the steady rubbing of his arms, just in case.

The figure was wearing a jacket with a blue or purple stripe. Material of the same colour fluttered from their hand. Alex stared. He blinked and stared again. There really was someone there. The figure had now reappeared, much closer, from behind a contour at the base of the mountain.

There was no need for Alex to think about the strain of forcing a shout from his dry throat or waving his sore arms. Such was his great joy that he yelled and waved his arms with an energy he didn't know he possessed.

A blue or purple stripe would mean either Jeff or Ricky. Alex would not have cared if it had been Seth or one of the Rock Men. So long as it was someone!

The figure had stopped and was looking round. He had heard him! Alex renewed his yells and waved his arms more frantically. The figure, facing Alex now, raised the scrap of material and waved. He had seen him! He gulped back a sob of relief. He had seen him and was coming! Alex was going to be rescued after all.

Then the figure turned away and disappeared from sight.

Alex stared in disbelief. It simply could not be true. Surely he would not leave Alex alone, trapped in the snow?

The relief, when Alex saw the figure reappear, left him feeling suddenly drained and weak. He could see now that it was Ricky and the reason for his disappearance became clear immediately. A second, smaller figure in a suit with a red stripe appeared behind him. He caught the gleam of golden hair. Callie. So Ricky had seen him and had then gone back to fetch Callie to help.

It was just as well Callie had been close by. Without a spade or any kind of instrument to dig with, it needed two of them to get Alex out of the snowdrift. Callie was afraid that Alex would suffer a reaction from the extreme cold. She searched in her backpack and gave him a capsule to swallow. He coughed and spluttered as it broke in his mouth and a fiery liquid scalded his throat.

Callie laughed. 'Don't worry, Alex. I'm not poisoning you. That should do you the world of good.'

That seemed to be just the beginning of the torture. Callie and Ricky rubbed Alex's legs until he could stand, and then they made him jog until the feeling came shooting back into them. When he could move more easily, Ricky suggested that they walk briskly to get his circulation going properly.

'Well, thank you both,' Alex grimaced as he moved painfully forward.

'It was a pleasure,' returned Callie, smiling.

Ricky did not smile. There was a time when he had had a smile and a joke for every occasion. Now he just nodded briefly. Alex remembered how he had been irritated by Ricky's non-stop jokes. He wished now that Ricky would make a joke. He felt guilty, realising that the delay he had caused might have cost Ricky the race if Ben or Jeff had been able to get ahead. He glanced at the summit of Anderloss. There was still no flag there. 'Ricky,' he said quietly, touching his arm, 'I really do appreciate what you've done. Thanks.'

Ricky forced a smile, but it did not reach his eyes. 'That's OK, Alex. Think nothing of it,' he said.

Alex felt reluctant to mention something that might cause an extra delay for Ricky, but he knew he had to tell the others about Seth.

'I wonder if I should go and take a look at him,' Callie pondered. 'If he's in worse shape than Alex thinks, we could get him to my spaceship and take him back to Base.'

'From the direction in which you approached Anderloss I should imagine your ship is a long way from where Alex crashed, isn't it, Callie?' Ricky objected.

'Well, yes,' admitted Callie. 'But perhaps I ought to look at Seth anyway.'

Alex did not know what to say. If Seth had some internal injury they were unaware of, it would be wrong not to get him help as soon as possible. Alex himself knew what it was like now to be desperately in need of help. He shuddered to think what would have happened if Ricky and Callie had not come along.

'Then there's you, Alex,' Callie continued. 'You're in no shape to finish the race. What do you think, Ricky?'

Ricky shifted impatiently from foot to foot. 'We're wasting time here. I think we . . .'

Alex was never to find out what Ricky would have said next. The bleeper on Ricky's radio cut him off midsentence. For a moment the three of them stared at each other in startled surprise, then Ricky tapped his wrist console. 'Yes? What is it?'

The answering voice was slightly distorted but the message was clear enough for all colour to drain from Alex's face.

'Can't contact Alex,' it said. 'Find him . . . urgent . . . contact Base . . . his parents . . . accident at Reba . . .'

Chapter ten

Ricky glanced quickly at Alex as Callie took his arm sympathetically. 'Do you want to speak to him? He's here now.'

Alex leaned forward to speak into the microphone. 'Alex?' the voice queried and the line went dead.

'Hello,' Alex said. 'Hello? This is Alex.' But, as he had expected, there was no reply.

'Alex,' Ricky said and his voice seemed to come from a long way away. 'We'll take my ship and go back to Base.'

Alex tried to clear his head. A nightmare kaleidoscope of pictures swirled through his mind. An earthquake . . . a fire . . . an explosion at Reba . . . His parents injured . . . dead . . . He closed his eyes and drew a hand across his forehead as if it would clarify his thoughts.

'No, it's all right, Ricky. I'd rather go by myself.'

'I'll come with you, Alex,' said Callie. 'You're in no state to go by yourself.'

'I'll go alone,' Alex said firmly, almost shouting.

Callie lowered her eyes and said nothing.

'Take my compass to get directions back to my ship,' offered Ricky. 'It's not far.'

'Thanks,' murmured Alex, taking the compass without

really seeing it. 'Say hello to the summit of Anderloss for me.'

Callie began to protest again. Alex silenced her with a drawn smile. 'You and Ricky have to finish the race, Callie. Somebody has to. Otherwise it's all been for nothing, hasn't it?' Turning to Ricky he added, 'I'll get somebody to fly your ship back. And I'll tell them about Seth.'

'Be careful then, Alex,' said Ricky, slapping him on the back. 'Don't worry about the ship. I can come back with Callie.'

'Yes, of course,' Callie agreed. 'All the best then, Alex.'

'Thanks,' responded Alex, turning away.

'I'll be praying for you,' Callie called after him.

Alex paused to give Callie a quick, quizzical glance over his shoulder. She was trying to smile but he could see tears brimming in her blue eyes. 'Thanks,' Alex said again and, setting Ricky's compass for the reading to the spaceship, he walked off without another backward glance.

As Ricky had said, the spaceship was not very far away. Alex entered the cockpit with mixed feelings. He would be glad to be able to find out exactly what had happened and to be on his way back but he was afraid of what he might learn. If something had happened to his parents, he did not know if he could take it.

With trembling hands he worked the controls of the ship's radio. Part of him was relieved when nothing happened at first then, as he tried again, he became frustrated and a surge of anger welled up inside him. What was wrong with the radio when he needed so desperately to use it to find out if his parents were all right? Alex gave an impatient tug at the wires and stared in disbelief as they came away in his hands. They had been cut. Why? One more strange incident in a series of strange incidents. What was going on in the Waste Zone?

A slight rustling sound behind him made him spin round. Nothing. Perhaps, after the incident with Seth, he was becoming over-sensitive. He turned back to the control panel. If he had to fly back to Base without a radio, then he was going to double-check that everything was in perfect working order. Yes. As far as he could see, everything was fine.

This time there was no mistaking the sound. There was a sudden small clatter as if something had been dropped. Alex sat perfectly still, listening. The silence which followed seemed full of tension, as if someone waited, holding their breath.

Alex slid his hand slowly, quietly to the laser gun in his pocket. He tensed, waiting to spin round at the slightest sound. It was hard to sit, waiting, while his imagination ran riot. Behind him there was a man creeping up on him with a knife . . . or Seth, miraculously recovered and now on this ship, stealthily crept forward to knock him out . . . or . . . He was just beginning to feel that he could sit still no longer when the sound came. It was quiet, very quiet – no more than a light footfall and a disturbance of air. Alex swung round, his laser gun pointing in the direction of the noise.

The sight that met Alex's eyes startled him. He almost dropped the gun. He did not know what he had expected to see but it had not been a Rock Man.

The Rock Man, looking less fierce in the alien environment of the ship, seemed as taken aback as Alex. One glance at him told Alex that he need not fear an attack from this strange, small creature. If anything, he was more afraid than Alex. He was dressed, not in the primitive clothes that the Rock Men in the cave had worn, but in a modern jumpsuit. He did not carry a spear but, like Alex, had a laser gun at his side. As Alex watched him he saw the grey hand reach slowly for the gun.

Alex raised his own gun, pointing it at the place between the tiny black eyes beneath the lowering brow. 'I wouldn't if I were you,' he said grimly.

The Rock Man's eyes widened as he glanced down from the purposeful set of Alex's face to the gun in his hand. In sheer panic he lunged towards the door. Alex had had no intention of firing and perhaps the Rock Man sensed that it was worth taking the risk to try to escape. Alex lowered the gun and, with an agonizing effort, threw himself after the Rock Man. He almost had him but his own left arm was not back to its full strength. The Rock Man was much nimbler than he had expected and twisted out of his grasp to dive for the doorway. Alex knew that if the small man left the ship he would not be able to catch him. He gathered the last reserves of his energy into a tremendous leap at the departing figure. This time he caught him by the right ankle and brought him crashing down on the floor.

The Rock Man struggled in a frenzy of fear. Alex hung on. He was at the limit of his strength and about to give up, when the Rock Man suddenly went limp.

'No shoot. Please. Mean no harm.'

Alex trained his gun on the quivering man. He did not trust him. The fact that he had spoken in Alex's own language, even though it was with a strong accent, had taken Alex by surprise. It did make things easier though. He felt uneasy doing it but Alex decided to take advantage of the man's fear. He spoke brusquely.

'I won't shoot if you talk. What were you doing,

breaking into this ship?'

Despite Alex's tone the man relaxed. Alex hoped he would be able to keep control of the situation.

'Me warn ship-master,' he said.

'Ship-master? You came to see Ricky?' Somehow the information did not quite ring true. 'Warn him about what?'

'You friend ship-master?' the Rock Man asked cautiously.

Alex thought the Rock Man was in no position to hold reservations about parting with his information. He admired his nerve.

'Yes. I'm Ricky's friend. Which is why I don't like anyone snooping round his ship.' Alex hoped he sounded aggressive. 'If you expect me to believe you were here to warn Ricky, you'd better have something worthwhile to be warning him about. I'm just asking one more time.' Alex raised his laser gun meaningfully. 'Warn him about what?'

'Warn ship-master about . . .' The Rock Man glanced round fearfully and lowered his voice. Finally he risked something, but it was no more than a whisper. Alex had to strain to catch it. 'Trap. Anderloss.'

'Trap?' Alex repeated wonderingly. 'On Anderloss?' His pulse quickened. It made sense. There was someone behind all the things that had gone wrong. How else could that someone eliminate the final competitors who were left standing against him but by setting a trap on Anderloss?

'Who?' Alex asked. 'Who set the trap?'

'Him want win race,' the Rock Man stated. He kept his voice low. 'Him try trap space cadets in cave.'

Alex began to feel excited. He attempted to keep his voice even. 'What is his name?'

'Name . . . ?' The Rock Man hesitated. The whites of his eyes showed, giving his grey face a grotesque look. 'His name Kensa – Boss Man.'

'Kensa?' repeated Alex, disappointed. 'Boss Man?' Who would the Rock Men call Boss Man? Was it someone he had never met or was it a name given by the Rock Men to one of his fellow competitors? After all, he had said that this Kensa, Boss Man, had wanted to win the race.

'Kensa?' Alex began. 'Is that . . . ?' Then he realised his mistake. In the fraction of a second that he had been distracted, wondering about the name, the Rock Man had made a dash for the door.

'Hey!' Alex yelled, aiming his gun. 'Stop!' The Rock Man was already through the door and dropping nimbly to the ground. He ran recklessly without looking back.

Alex lowered his gun, the energy suddenly draining out of him. He watched until the Rock Man had disappeared from sight, then he closed the door and walked slowly over to the cockpit. He slumped into the pilot's seat.

What was he to do now? Go back to Base to find out what had happened at Reba? He longed more than anything now to find out if his parents were all right. But the Rock Man had spoken of a trap on Anderloss. Callie and Ricky were climbing Anderloss now. Perhaps Ben and Jeff were on Anderloss too. Could he let them climb without warning them about the trap?

He thought for a moment about Ricky and Callie. Ricky had been there when he needed help twice now. Once in the cavern when he had blacked out, and then when he had fallen in the snow-drift. Callie had been ready to help anyone she could all through this race. It was a strange attitude when he thought about it. She must want the place in the SESU or she would not have got this far through to the final. Yet she did not seem to mind stopping to help people when she could have been getting ahead. She reminded him in a way of someone . . .

He remembered, with a jolt, her parting words. 'I'll be praying for you.' It couldn't be that someone as bright and intelligent as Callie believed the same nonsense his father believed? For some reason he could not quite put his finger on, his heart sank at that thought. And yet the thought was strangely comforting. It felt as if, while he stepped out into danger, there was someone behind him, covering him with a laser gun, protecting him from harm.

Still he hesitated. Even the Rock Man's warning about a trap might itself be a trap. Ricky and Callie might be fine and going after them might be risky in itself. He seemed to have had more than his fair share of danger already in this race. Meanwhile, his parents might need him desperately. Perhaps they had been fatally injured. This thought hit Alex as if a yawning chasm had opened at his feet, but he forced himself to follow it through. If that happened then he might be able to reach them in time to see them just once more.

Alex leaned back in the seat and stared unseeing at the desolate landscape of the waste land beyond the cockpit window. For a moment he stopped struggling to make sense of it all and let his mind go blank.

'I'll be praying for you,' Callie had said.

He closed his eyes. A feeling of calm unexpectedly washed over him. It was all right. Everything was going to work out. He had only to move in the right direction and the rest would take care of itself. Or be taken care of!

79

He opened his eyes again and gave a yell of excitement. He was beginning to see things more clearly. Once his mind had stopped spinning round like a hamster on a wheel he could now see the obvious thing he had missed before.

It was not going back to Anderloss that was the trap. It was going back to Base. He was suddenly as sure as if he had received a radio message to tell him that there had been no accident at Reba, no danger to his parents. The radio message Ricky had received was the trap, neatly sprung to eliminate Alex from the race.

Why he had not realised this sooner he could not imagine now. But Ricky and Callie had not seen through it either. That call must have been a hoax because they were out of radio contact with Base. The only way someone could make contact with Base was by radio on their ship. And this was for emergencies only, to call for help, not to receive messages.

Someone wanted Alex out of the way. Callie and Ricky were immediately eliminated from suspicion. Both of them had been there when Ricky had received the radio message. It could not have been Seth, who was lying unconscious in Alex's ship. It could have been Jeff though Alex found it hard to tie in with Jeff's recent actions. Alex also felt that there was something about the call which, if he could put his finger on it, would point clearly to the hoaxer. Meanwhile as far as he could see, there was only one person it could have been. Quiet, hesitant, harmless Ben.

The thought was ludicrous but perhaps that was because Ben had played his part so cleverly. Alex remembered how, in the cavern, Ben had spoken to the Rock Men in their own language. Perhaps there was another side to him, a dangerous, ruthless side that none of them had seen. He might stop at nothing. He thought he had eliminated Alex. What would he do to make sure he reached the mountaintop ahead of Callie and Ricky? They might, even at this moment, be walking into his final trap. There was only one way, it seemed to Alex, to stop Ben – if it was not already too late. Alex must hurry back to face whatever treacherous events were unfolding on the wintry slopes of Anderloss.

Chapter eleven

A silence, deep as the untrodden snow, hung over Anderloss. There was no one in sight. No sign of life. Neither was there a flag at the summit, Alex noted with relief as he squinted, shielding his eyes against the glare of the snow. There was still a chance he would arrive in time.

As he walked to Anderloss, Alex realised how much the accidents, especially his fall into the snow-drift, had affected him. He was so tired. The arm which he had injured in the spaceship crash was now throbbing constantly. His short time in Ricky's spaceship, and the hot drink he had hurriedly brewed in the galley before setting out again, had warmed him and revived him somewhat, but he was badly in need of a proper rest. As he reached the lower slopes of the mountain, his limbs were aching. By the time he had climbed a short way – an exercise which he had been able to take in his stride while training – he was already battling with fatigue. When he was what he estimated to be half-way up the mountain, he began to wonder how much longer he could go on. And still there was no sight or sound of the others.

Each step became a huge effort. His stiff legs almost refused to bend, when he reached a broad ledge which stretched in a narrow shelf round the curve of the mountain. Alex lowered himself into a sitting position on a bare patch of ground and leaned back against the jagged rock face.

He knew he dared not rest for long. Already the frosty mountain air was biting into him. But, despite the cold, there was the danger of falling asleep. It would be so easy to let go, to slip into a peaceful place free from cold and pain and tiredness. Easy and perhaps fatal.

Alex dragged himself reluctantly to his feet, stamping and flapping his arms to gain some semblance of warmth. He forced his mind to concentrate on something other than his aches and pains. Where, he asked himself, were the others? Why were none of them in sight?

If Ben had set a trap and Ricky, Callie and perhaps Jeff had fallen into it, that would explain why none of them were climbing the slopes of Anderloss. But if that had happened, where was Ben?

Alex paced back and forth, trying to keep warm and to ease the stiffness in his legs, while he scanned the mountain slopes above the plateau, looking for the easiest route to continue his ascent.

Another thought occurred to him. If he had been wrong and Ben was not the traitor, if there really was someone called Kensa, then Ben too could have walked into a trap. He could not imagine what kind of trap would catch all four of them.

It was still his gut feeling that the traitor was one of the competitors in the race and not an unknown stranger. So, if Ben had succeeded in eliminating Ricky, Callie and Jeff from the race, Ben must be somewhere on the slopes of Anderloss. If Alex could force himself to finish the climb then, as the paths to the summit converged near the pinnacle, he would be sure to meet

Ben. Alex shuddered at the thought. How could he, in his weakened condition, face the stronger and ruthless Ben? This Ben would not be the meek, hesitant person he thought he knew, but a terrifying stranger.

His pacing took him round the curve of the rock face to another side of Anderloss screened from the slope he had been climbing. As he rounded the sharp angle of the rocks the thought uppermost in his mind was that at any minute now he might see Ben. If he did, Alex was not sure what he would do – follow him up the mountain, or return to the safety of Ricky's ship and fly back to Base?

The moment the new slope of the mountain came into view, Alex saw the figure. High up, almost out of his range of vision, a climber was steadily scaling the steep mountainside. Alex could just make out the flash of orange stripe on the jacket. He realised now that, despite all his speculation, he had not actually expected to see anyone. He had thought that he would climb to the summit of Anderloss alone.

Alex stared at the small figure, rubbed his eyes and stared again. His heart gave a sudden leap of joy. In his first fearful glance he had been mistaken. The stripe on the jacket was not orange. It was red. The lonely figure nearing the summit was not Ben but Callie.

With an ease which surprised him, Alex moved to the far left of the ledge. The sight of Callie had done more for him than any amount of ointment or medicine to give a new energy to his aching limbs.

Yes, it was definitely Callie. As he strained his eyes he caught the gleam of her golden hair. She was not very far from the summit of Anderloss but between her and the mountain peak there lay an obstacle, an overhang of rock, heavy with snow. Alex could not see how she could pass it if she continued on the path she was climbing now. She showed no signs of moving sideways but he was sure that sooner or later she was going to have to veer either to the left or right to get round the overhang. Alex craned his neck to scan the slope on the far left of the overhang, wondering if the terrain there would make for easier climbing.

Two figures, one almost parallel with Callie, one higher up the slope, were climbing the mountain. The surprise of seeing Ricky and Ben, even though he had been looking for them, almost made Alex lose his footing. He moved quickly back onto a wider, safer area of the ledge. In doing so he lost sight of the climbers, though he had a clear picture of them in his mind's eye. Ricky had been level with Callie and Ben a short distance above them both.

Alex returned his gaze to the spot below the overhang where Callie was still climbing steadily upwards. His mind raced. The picture he had just seen looked so normal and innocent. Ben had been ahead, but only a short distance ahead. It did not look as if he could be leading Ricky, close behind him, into a trap.

Callie was now at last beginning to move to the left. She could not see either Ben or Ricky from where she was and probably had no idea they were so close. By the time she manoeuvred round the overhang, both of them would probably have gained ground. Whereas now she was equal second with Ricky and stood a chance of catching up with Ben if he faltered, moving sideways would mean she would fall into third place behind Ricky. It looked at the moment as if the winner of the race was going to be Ben.

A slight movement caught Alex's eye, making him look higher up the mountain. He half expected to see

Ben climbing into sight. What he actually saw made his heart leap into his throat. It took a few seconds for his brain to accept the evidence of his eyes. A figure walked out, seemingly from nowhere, onto the overhang. It was a Rock Man. Behind him a second figure came into sight. Jeff! Alex hardly had time to be surprised at Jeff's sudden appearance, and to wonder what he and the Rock Man were doing on the overhang, when the Rock Man lifted his arm and threw something. Alex watched it arc high into the air before it thudded down into the white expanse of snow between Alex and the overhang. The realisation of what he was doing hit Alex a few seconds before the explosion. There was a thunderous crack then the deep rumble of falling snow. The Rock Man had started an avalanche!

The next moment Alex had no time to think of anything but staying alive as a landslide of falling snow, strewn with stones, rushed down the mountain slope towards him. He slammed himself quickly against the rock face, finding a hand-hold where the rock dipped slightly between the ledge and the cliff face. There he clung tightly while snow and falling rock piled onto the ledge. He gritted his teeth as flying rocks and solid chunks of snow pelted him. He buried his face into the angle of the rock face and the ground, hoping it would soon be over.

As abruptly as it had begun it stopped. Alex lay still for a moment under the weight of snow which covered him like a blanket, and listened to the awesome silence. Slowly he eased himself up through the cold, snowy deposit of the avalanche and got shakily to his feet. Where the wide ledge had been before there was now an expanse of snow and rock. Alex clambered over the uneven surface until he had a clear view of the mountain face. He raised his eyes, searching the slope below the overhang, hoping to catch a reassuring glimpse of a small figure with a brave red stripe on her jacket. It seemed to him that the avalanche had started from below the spot where Callie was climbing but he could not be sure. If he was wrong . . . He dared not follow that disturbing train of thought.

The overhang was now empty. Jeff and the Rock Man had gone. This was something else Alex could not understand – why had Jeff been on the plateau with the Rock Man? It looked as if he had been wrong. It might not be Ben, after all, who was the traitor. This latest, alarming incident pointed to Jeff. But Alex was wary now of jumping to any conclusions. He pushed the conflicting ideas to the back of his mind and forced himself to concentrate on the climb.

Drifts of disturbed snow shifted in powdery clouds down the mountainside, making it difficult for Alex to see clearly. He bit his lip, straining to see, anxious to begin the climb to where he had last seen Callie. If he could locate her position before he set off it would save him time in the long run because, from the vantage point of the ledge, he could see the breadth of the mountain slope. When he climbed, the view would be obscured by the twists and turns of the trail. The thought that he might not see her at all, that she might be buried under a shroud of snow, filled him with a gnawing dread.

A flash of memory taunted him. Callie with her blue eyes filled with concern. 'I'll be praying for you,' she had said. Staring at the deserted mountain slope, feeling helpless, with an awful fear gnawing away at him, Alex wished he could pray for Callie. He wished he really thought there was a God somewhere out there who listened to people, who looked out for them, who wanted to help them. A God who could help Callie.

Perhaps there was. He remembered his desperate cry for help in the snowdrift. Just after that, Ricky and Callie had come along and he had been rescued. This may have been coincidence; but a small part of him, that he was reluctant to recognise, longed to believe that it had not been coincidence but an answer to his terrified prayer.

'Please let her be all right,' he whispered and waited. As the moments dragged by with agonizing slowness he felt anger building up inside him as the mountain stayed an expanse of unbroken whiteness except for the grey of the rocks. What was the use of asking for help from a God who didn't exist or, if he did exist, couldn't or wouldn't do anything? He took a step forward to begin his futile climb up to the overhang. He lifted his face to the grey sky and shouted, 'Callie believed in you. I'm sure she did. Why didn't you help her? Don't you care?'

His words fell into silence. The sky remained blank and indifferent. Alex now felt foolish as well as frightened and angry. He kicked ineffectually at the snow, knowing it was a childish gesture.

As suddenly as the surge of negative emotions had taken hold of him they left him again, drained. He must find Callie, whatever had happened to her. If she was in a state to need help, he must help her. He must pull himself together if he was going to be of use to anyone.

He began his ascent of the mountain, moving cautiously, aware that the going underfoot would be more treacherous now as it was hard to detect pockets of deep snow. He looked up for one last time at the clear mountain slope before a twist in the trail would take it out of his view. It was then, for just a matter of seconds, that an absolute stillness descended over the mountain.

He could see the whole glistening panorama in front of him with amazing clarity. He could pick out a faint slash of red in the unending expanse of whiteness below the overhang.

Before he could feel any emotion of relief, in the same brief fraction of time, a movement on the over-hang caught his eye. There were two figures, grappling together. Locked in a fierce struggle, they teetered towards the edge. Abruptly one of the figures moved backwards and Alex saw, to his horror, the other figure, a flash of orange on his jacket, fall over the edge. Like a diver in slow motion, he somersaulted through the air to land with a thud in the snow far below.

Chapter twelve

The climb seemed to take forever. Twice Alex stepped into a hidden pocket of snow and had to scramble to regain his footing. Several times during the course of his ascent he paused, waiting until his ragged breathing was even before yelling Callie's name, then Ricky's. Hopes that Ricky, higher up and round the curve of the mountain, would hear him, were faint but he had to try. There was no way that he could help an injured Ben on his own and he doubted that Callie, even if she heard him, would be strong enough to help; but he had to believe that help would come from somewhere or he could not possibly keep going on this well-nigh impossible climb.

The hopelessness of the situation stabbed at his mind from time to time like a chilling sliver of ice. He could not stop himself thinking of all the problems, not to mention the possible danger. He had not seen the figure grappling with Ben on the overhang clearly. Had it been a Rock Man? Or had it been Jeff? Jeff, who had risked his life going back into the cave to rescue Seth? No. He couldn't believe that. But someone was behind all the things that had gone wrong. Someone was telling the Rock Men what to do. Kensa. The Boss Man. The one who would stop at nothing to win the race.

Alex also considered the possibility that there might be more than one Rock Man on the mountainside. Even a single Rock Man lying in wait, perhaps armed, would present a danger which Alex in his present state would not be fit to cope with. For the sake of his peace of mind, Alex talked himself into believing that the Rock Man had not seen him and would now be making his way back down the mountain, while Jeff would be climbing to the top.

Or they might both be climbing up after Ricky.

Alex dragged his thoughts back to the effort of his own climb. He had lost sight of the places where Ben had fallen and where he had last seen Callie. All he could do was concentrate on the next foothold, on tracing the pathway through the drift of snow and rock which obscured it.

His only plan was to reach Ben, check that he was still breathing and see how badly he was injured. After that he would have to leave Ben to go and look for Callie. Maybe he would then have to leave them both to find Ricky. How he and Ricky would get Ben, and perhaps Callie, down the mountainside to a ship, he dared not think. He might, if he could not find Ricky, have to leave his two injured friends and take Ricky's spaceship back to Base.

And what if Ricky, unaware of all that had been happening, had returned to his ship and left? If Alex went back to the spot where Ricky's spaceship had been and found it gone, what then?

Concentrate, he told himself. Just concentrate. One thing at a time. Reach Ben. That's the first thing. Just get to Ben.

As he pressed on through the deep snow, Alex promised himself that never again would he walk into an unknown situation so ill-prepared. All the training for the race, which he felt he had handled so competently, had not sharpened his mind enough to deal with the unforeseen crises he had faced in the Waste Zone. It seemed as if disaster after disaster had dogged the competitors from the start. They had not been trained for any of this.

As for the actual climbing of Anderloss, Alex felt sure that the organisers of the race had envisaged a straightforward climb up one of the mountain's many paths. Neither Alex nor the others had been trained or issued with equipment for climbing in these conditions. There was no provision either for more than the basics of first aid. Certainly Alex had nothing for helping anyone in the condition in which he expected to find Ben. Some provision should have been made for contacting Base on their wrist consoles in case of emergency too. Not that that would have done Alex any good now, since his wrist console had been smashed. He thought he would make all these points when he got back to Base. If he got back to Base.

Coming up over the brow of a snowy incline, Alex's heart skipped a beat. A short distance ahead of him, like a bundle of rags huddled in the snow, lay the still form of Ben. Alex hurried towards him, half-running where the snow allowed him, stumbling in his haste.

Ben had fallen on his side, with one leg twisted under him at an awkward angle. His face, drained of colour, was almost as white as the snow. But he was still breathing. Alex bent over him and could see no obvious signs of injury apart from the twisted leg. He felt a little uneasy at the shallowness of Ben's breathing and the chill of his skin. He had obviously been losing warmth rapidly since his fall.

Alex felt a rush of anger and frustration that he could do nothing for him. He could not cover him with anything to keep him warm. He dared not give him any medication, unsure as he was if there were internal injuries. He would just have to leave Ben as he was to go and look for Callie. A terrible fear nagged at him. If he turned his back on Ben now and walked away, Ben might die. Alex knew he had no choice but all the same he felt he was deserting him.

As he levered himself back onto his feet, a flicker of hope sparked briefly in Alex's mind. Perhaps he was not alone to cope with this. When he had yelled angrily at Callie's God – had it been a coincidence that, just after his desperate cry, he had glimpsed Callie on the mountain? And before that, when he had been trapped in the snow-drift, had it been a coincidence too that Ricky had come along? Perhaps, just perhaps, this God really was there, really did care?

Doubts sprang to Alex's mind, ready to niggle away at the blossoming flower of hope. If there was a God who did care and could help, why hadn't he stopped the Rock Man? It was because of the Rock Man that Ben was barely alive, and who knew what had happened to Callie! Alex struggled against the thoughts that snuffed out the glimmer of hope and spoke quickly before he could change his mind.

'I don't understand any of this properly but, if you really are there and you really did help me, please do something for Ben now. Please look after him. Don't let him die. And Callie – let her be OK. And . . .' He paused, seeking to put the enormity of his problem into words. '. . . Help me. I don't think this is something I can manage. I have to find a way somehow though I can't really see how. Help us all. Please?'

With a last look at Ben's pale face, Alex turned away and began walking resolutely up the mountain. He hoped he was heading in the right direction.

The terrain on this part of the mountain was quite jagged so it was hard going for Alex. It was, he realised, lucky for Ben that he had fallen lower down the slope where the ground was smooth and blanketed with a deep layer of newly fallen snow. If Ben had fallen where Alex was walking now, where rocks protruded from the snow like jagged teeth . . . Alex shuddered. He did not like to pursue the thought.

The next minute all thoughts of Ben were completely wiped from his mind. He thought he glimpsed a sudden movement behind a ridge further up the mountain. He stopped and ran his eyes over the spot, but there was no sign of movement now. His nerves must be more on edge than he thought if he was beginning to imagine things. He walked on, scrambling over an uneven outcrop of rocks. Looking up suddenly, he caught sight of the movement again. He knew this time that he had seen something, someone, moving down the mountainside towards him. But the glimpse had been as quick as the blink of an eye. He could not be sure who or what he had seen. An unreasonable hope told him that it was Ricky. He had seen the accident, seen where Ben had fallen and was coming down to help. Cold common sense told him it was more likely to be the Rock Man. It was no use saying he was not afraid. Ben was injured, and perhaps Callie was too because of a Rock Man. There was no knowing what he would do to Alex.

Alex tried to still his pounding heart and racing mind. He must think clearly. He moved to a spot where he would catch a glimpse of the unknown figure as it came over the next ridge, then crouched down, waiting, his hand poised to reach for his laser gun.

He did not have long to wait. The figure came into view once more and this time, because of the slope of the ground, stayed in sight for longer. It was much nearer now and he could make out the colour of its hair and clothing though the features were still a blur.

For a long moment Alex stood and stared then, as the figure began to disappear from sight again he leapt to his feet and yelled, 'Callie! Callie!'

The figure stopped in its tracks. He could hardly believe it. It really was Callie. She was turning her head, trying to locate him. He felt that the grin stretched across his face was so wide she ought to be able to see it from where she stood. He yelled again, waving his arms. This time she saw him. She waved back, then disappeared again.

Alex stayed where he was, waiting for her to reach him as they would need to go back down the mountain together to where Ben lay. Callie bobbed into view and disappeared again a few more times before she finally reached him. As he waited, he leaned back against the rock, trying to grasp the fact that she really was all right.

When at last she was standing there in front of him, Alex found he could not tell Callie of the feelings which had shaken him so deeply. But he could not stop grinning, and the joy at seeing her alive and well sparkled in his eyes.

'I'm so pleased to see you, Alex,' Callie greeted him, smiling back. Then the smile wavered and she shivered slightly. 'Wasn't it awful, Alex, the avalanche? I saw it start just below where I was climbing and . . .' She faltered and bit her lip. 'I . . . I saw someone fall, – from higher up the mountain.'

Alex saw that, although his fears that Callie had been

harmed by the avalanche were unfounded, she was still badly shaken. The climb down the mountain through the debris and fresh drifts of snow must have been gruelling. He hated to have to break the news to her that it was Ben who had fallen, but there was no time to waste.

'I've seen the person who fell, Callie.' Alex spoke quickly, hoping he sounded matter-of-fact. 'He's alive but injured.'

Callie's eyes widened in anxiety. 'Who is it?' she asked in a whisper.

'Ben,' Alex said.

It was typical of Callie that she did not waste time with unnecessary questions. The colour drained from her face. 'Show me,' she said.

At least Ben seemed no worse when they reached him. Callie examined him expertly and quickly. 'It's just his leg I think. That's broken. He may have concussion and, of course, there's the danger of internal bleeding. I think the biggest danger at the moment is the cold. We need to get him to a spaceship as quickly as possible and back to Base.'

Alex nodded. 'I don't think you and I can get him down alone. We need Ricky. If you stay with Ben, I'll climb up to see if I can find him.'

A faint smile came to Callie's lips. 'You do like doing things the hard way, don't you, Alex! Why climb when you can contact him by radio?'

Alex grimaced. 'My radio's broken,' he said.

'But mine isn't,' replied Callie still with the ghost of a smile. She touched her wrist console and made contact with Ricky.

Alex wondered if there was a hint of impatience in Ricky's voice as he answered. He was almost at the summit, he said, but, of course, he would come down at once. It would take some time.

'Warn him to look out for Rock Men – and Jeff,' Alex told Callie quickly as the thought of ambush occurred to him. Callie gave him a puzzled look but passed the message on to Ricky.

'Well, he's coming but I don't know how long it will take him to get here.' Callie's gaze rested anxiously on Ben's still body. 'What did you mean, "Warn him about the Rock Men and Jeff"?' she added, lifting her eyes to look at Alex curiously.

Alex would have preferred to keep that particular problem from Callie. There was already enough for her to worry about. But it had been important to warn Ricky, so now he had to tell her exactly what had happened since he had left her, and what he had seen on the overhang.

Callie shook her head wonderingly. 'Jeff!' she said. 'I can't believe it.' She was quiet for a moment before she spoke again. 'I'm glad your parents are all right anyway,' she went on, typically picking out the one positive thing in all that he had told her – the heart-warming feeling Alex had experienced, knowing that his parents were safe. Alex sensed there was more Callie would have liked to have said, but she gave him a quiet smile, touched his hand in a brief gesture of reassurance and then fell silent. Neither of them really felt like talking any more.

Time dragged by with painful slowness as they waited for Ricky to arrive. Callie suggested that they crouch down on either side of Ben to give him as much body warmth as possible. While that idea lessened Alex's anxiety over Ben, it meant that he himself was exposed to the mountain chill. It worried him that Callie would be suffering the same icy numbness. They would have to warm up before they were fit to get Ben down the mountainside.

It was a great relief when at last Ricky came in sight. After he had seen for himself the state Ben was in, they discussed briefly how they could get him down the mountain.

'How about the flags?' Callie suggested. 'Could we make some kind of stretcher?'

'Afraid mine's on top of Anderloss,' Ricky said. Alex glanced at him quickly. So he had carried on up to the summit before coming down to help them. Now was not the time, he told himself, to pass any judgments. He must remember that Ricky had not taken advantage of the head start he had gained in leaving the caves before the others. He had also delayed climbing Anderloss when he rescued Alex from the snowdrift. Perhaps Alex only imagined that he detected a smirk in Ricky's voice.

In the end they made a splint for Ben's broken leg out of Callie's flag. Ricky and Alex took the bulk of Ben's weight, with Callie supporting when there was a particular hurdle to cross. Pausing occasionally to rest and to change places, they painstakingly made their way down the mountain.

In all that time, even with the unavoidable jolting, Ben did not stir. Alex's fear that it would be too late by the time they got him back to Base, grew stronger. It was a great relief when they reached Ricky's ship.

They had to lay Ben down on the floor, but Callie found some blankets to put under him and cover him. She crouched down beside him in the cramped quarters of the cockpit while Ricky navigated the ship and Alex sat alongside him in the co-pilot's seat.

They had already started the journey back to Base when Callie gave a cry of alarm. 'Alex! He's stopped breathing!'

Alex was out of his seat and beside her in an instant. He looked in shocked disbelief from Callie's stricken eyes to the deathly mask of stillness that was Ben's face.

'Right!' Alex said out loud, surprising himself. 'This is the big one. God . . . Lord God . . . or whatever, can you do something fast? Please. You've got Ben this far. Don't let him die now.'

He looked at Callie who was staring at him, wide-eyed. 'I'm going to try mouth-to-mouth,' he said.

'Right,' Callie managed. 'I'll carry on praying.'

There was no response from the still form on the floor. Alex steeled himself to remain calm, to keep going automatically through the technique of resuscitation. It was nearly his undoing when he remembered a moment on the training course when he'd actually had to practise on Ben. 'Hope we don't have to do this one on the race,' Ben had joked. 'I'll die if we do!'

'Don't die,' Alex whispered. He took a deep breath and began the process all over again.

'Alex,' Callie whispered.

Her voice seemed to reach him from a distance, down a long tunnel of numbness and despair.

'Alex, I think he's breathing.'

Alex lifted his head and looked closely at Ben. There was, as Callie had said, a faint flutter of breath. Alex felt the tears fill in his eyes. His vision of Ben blurred.

Callie leaned over to hug him. 'I think he's going to make it,' she said.

Chapter thirteen

As he dressed for the banquet at which the winner of the race was to be officially announced, Alex thought back to that harrowing return flight to Base. He remembered the feeling of having stepped out over the edge of a bottomless pit when Callie had told him Ben had stopped breathing. Then there had come the incredible feeling of soaring, of having a dark sky burst into sunlight around him, when Ben had started to breathe again.

The medicare team had been amazed that Ben had survived in those wintry conditions with a broken leg and concussion. Alex, Callie and Ricky had received their fair share of praise for rescuing him.

'Are you ready, Alex?' his mother called from the other side of the door. 'It's nearly time to go if we're not to be late.'

Alex had mixed feelings about going to the banquet. He was looking forward to seeing Callie and Ben again, but he was finding the acute disappointment of not having won hard to handle. He thought he had come to terms with the frustration of failure but somehow, despite the fact that he had saved him from the snowdrift, Alex felt very uneasy with the thought that it was Ricky who had won.

Most of all he dreaded seeing Jeff. He and Callie had

talked about whether or not Alex should report what he had seen on the overhang. They had finally decided that they would see what happened at the banquet and try to talk to Commander Rudge privately afterwards.

There was not the same urgency in voicing their doubts about Jeff as there would have been if he had won.

Alex brought his thoughts back to the present as his mother called a second time.

'Yes, Mum. I'm as ready as I'll ever be,' he answered ruefully, running a final comb through his hair.

The first person Alex saw in the banquet room, crowded with people resplendent in uniforms and evening dress, was Seth. Most of the gathering stood in small groups, chatting and helping themselves to drinks and small appetising snacks, from trays which some of the younger SESU cadets were handing round. Seth was in a group in the far corner of the room. He looked very serious and intent as he listened to an older man in SESU uniform.

'Creep!' thought Alex. Alex had heard that Seth had arrived back safely at Base in the ship Callie would have used if she had not returned in Ricky's ship. Beyond that he had no further details. He had been told that Seth had been seen wandering cheerfully about in the leisure area, so Alex knew he was all right. He managed to avoid Seth and hoped that he would be able to avoid him for most of the evening. Alex could see now that Seth had recovered fully from the spaceship crash. He knew he shouldn't be thinking that way, but he thought Seth ought to be the one with the broken leg.

'Hi, Alex. Isn't this exciting!' Callie's cheerful voice at his elbow made him turn.

Callie, in a pale pink ankle length dress, with her long

hair loose about her shoulders, looked very pretty, very different from the workmanlike Callie he had known during training and the race. Her face glowed and her eyes sparkled with excitement as she glanced round the room.

'There's Ben!' she exclaimed with pleasure and waved to attract his attention.

Ben, his right leg in plaster, came hobbling across the room to them on crutches. He negotiated groups of people, trailing evening gowns and cadets with trays, as if it were an obstacle race.

'Well, congratulations, Ben!' said Callie, laughing. 'I think you won *that* race anyway.'

'Not bad, was it,' smiled Ben, flexing himself on his crutches. 'Comes with practice, you know. And now for something really spectacular . . .' He glanced from Callie to Alex with a raised eyebrow. Lifting his crutches with a flourish, he balanced on one leg, then wobbled dangerously till Callie forced him to put both crutches to the ground.

Alex joined in Callie's infectious laughter. All the tensions he had felt about the evening suddenly slipped away from him. It was good to be with two close friends, two very special people, who didn't seem to mind about losing. It looked like it was going to be one of those evenings when things which weren't that funny were going to reduce them to helpless laughter. It was going to be an evening to enjoy after all.

Then catching sight of the expression on Callie's face, Alex felt a bubble of laughter well up inside him. Her mouth had fallen open and her eyes were wide with surprise as she stared speechlessly across the room.

'Alex, look!' she gasped in dismay.

Alex turned in the direction she had indicated, fully

expecting to see at least a ghost. What he actually saw was Jeff! Jeff wearing SESU uniform.

It was impossible. Jeff could not be wearing SESU uniform! Alex felt the blood rush to his head and, for a moment or two, found it difficult to think clearly. Even if Jeff had won, he should not be wearing the uniform until after the official announcement and his enrolment in the SESU. But Jeff had not won. It was Ricky who claimed he had been the first to plant his flag on the summit of Anderloss. Alex could not imagine what was going on. He only knew that he had to speak urgently to Commander Rudge.

'Did Jeff win then?' asked Ben, bewilderment in his voice.

Perhaps Jeff had sensed their eyes on him, for he looked across the room, smiled and waved. Alex could see him excusing himself from the group he was with and making his way across the room to join them. Alex looked round desperately for Commander Rudge. He was nowhere to be seen. There was still time for Alex to leave the group before Jeff reached them, but he wondered if he should stay and confront Jeff with the incident he had witnessed on the overhang. Then it was too late to make a decision as Jeff reached Callie's side. Ben came out with his question again.

'Jeff, did you win the race?'

Jeff looked puzzled for a moment before he realised the cause of their confusion, then he laughed. 'The uniform, you mean? Well, that's a long story. If you're wondering about the winner, I think it's probably all right to tell you now that it was Seth's flag they found at the summit of Anderloss.'

'Seth?' questioned Alex, his voice rising in disbelief. 'Are you sure?'

104

But Jeff refused to say any more. 'Just hold on a few minutes and everything will be explained,' was all he would say.

Alex caught Callie's eye. She looked as mystified as he was. This new information was completely baffling. They had both heard Ricky say that he planted his flag on the summit. Another puzzle was Jeff's behaviour. He was being so friendly, it was hard to believe that he had deliberately tried to harm them. Everything's about to be explained, he had said. Alex doubted it but he would wait and see. He could always speak to Commander Rudge later.

Commander Rudge finally appeared. Alex caught sight of him mingling with the guests. Shortly after that, the Commander invited everyone to take their seats at tables beautifully laid with shining glassware and gleaming cutlery. Alex was pleased to find that he was seated with Ben and Callie. However, though the table was laid for five, the other two seats were unoccupied. Alex wondered briefly why all the competitors had not been seated together. He could see Ricky and Seth at a table on the far side of the room.

One of the senior SESU officers called for order. The buzz of excited chatter subsided and an expectant hush fell over the room. Commander Rudge came to stand on a carpeted podium which had been erected in the centre of the room.

To Alex's surprise Jeff slipped into the seat next to his. He smiled briefly at Alex, then turned his attention to Commander Rudge. Alex forced himself to concentrate on the Commander's opening words.

'And now we come to the moment we've all been waiting for,' smiled the Commander. 'I would like to announce the winner of the special race which was staged last week – the winner of the place on the Space Explorers' Special Unit team!'

Chapter fourteen

Alex glanced quickly at Jeff, trying to gauge his reaction. But Jeff sat there looking as cool and aloof as he had when they first knew him.

'But first of all,' Commander Rudge continued. 'I have some very grave and distressing things to say. Two of the six competitors are unfortunately disqualified from the race.'

There was a unified gasp of dismay throughout the room. A cold wave of fear washed over Alex. He had not gone to Ben's aid when Ben had called him on the radio for help. He had crashed his ship. Now he thought of it, he seemed to have got continually into trouble. There wasn't much he had done right until the end when he had helped rescue Ben.

'Two people,' the Commander was saying, 'have committed serious breaches of the rules.'

Alex thought suddenly of his parents sitting two tables away. How could he bear to be disgraced in front of them? He wished he could get up and leave the room. Instead he sat frozen, numb with dismay. He had no idea whose the other name would be, but he was very much afraid that the first person the Commander was going to name was Alex himself.

There was complete silence now in the room, then

Alex heard Commander Rudge's voice continue, low and troubled, as if he were speaking from the far end of a long tunnel, '. . . and have behaved in a disgraceful manner. I regret to announce that Seth Morcombe and Ricky Beckstrom are hereby disqualified from the race.'

Ricky! Alex sat at the table stunned. Now that he came to think of it, it was no great surprise to hear Seth's name mentioned. But Ricky! After the first stab of shock, relief washed over him, leaving him feeling suddenly weak.

'You OK, Alex?' asked a voice filled with concern. Alex lifted his eyes to see Jeff looking at him anxiously. Callie and Ben were staring in disbelief at Commander Rudge.

'Yes.' Alex found it hard to talk. 'Fine. It's such a shock, isn't it, Seth and Ricky being disqualified like that?'

'No, not really,' replied Jeff enigmatically.

Alex glanced at him in surprise, but could read nothing in the calm profile turned towards Commander Rudge. The Commander was speaking to Seth and Ricky. 'I'll talk to you boys later,' he said sternly.

'And now, ladies and gentlemen.' Commander Rudge projected his voice over the hubbub that had started at his announcement and a startled silence fell over the room. 'It gives me great pleasure to announce the winner, though any one of the remaining contestants . . .'

'But I won!' Ricky's voice cut rudely into the Commander's words. Alex glanced across the room. Seth was slumped in his chair, subdued for once, but Ricky was on his feet. 'I planted my flag first on Anderloss.' He turned accusingly to point at Jeff. 'Why is he in SESU uniform? I'd like to know who's been spreading

108

lies about me. I was the one who won!'

'Sit down, Mr Beckstrom, if you please,' said the Commander icily. 'The flag found at the summit was actually one Mr Morcombe claims to have planted. That is something we will discuss later in private.' Seth remained motionless, his head down. The Commander held Ricky's gaze steadily. 'I am well aware of *all* your actions in the Waste Zone. No one has been spreading lies. I will talk to you later,' he said.

Watching Ricky, Alex saw a change come over him at the Commander's words. All the fight seemed to go out of him and a sullenness crept into his face. Obviously the Commander's words had meant something to Ricky that he alone understood. He sat down abruptly, glaring mutinously at the table in front of him.

'As I was saying,' the Commander continued, managing somehow with his tone of voice and relaxed expression to restore a sense of harmony to the proceedings. 'It gives me great pleasure . . .' he beamed, 'very great pleasure to announce a worthy winner.'

He paused, making sure that he had the attention of the whole room. Alex glanced round at the sea of faces all turned expectantly towards Commander Rudge. Ricky, despite his bad-mannered outburst, had been forgotten already. Alex felt his stomach churn and his heartbeat quicken as the Commander began to speak again.

'The winner is – Ben Ortlund.'

Ben!

The room burst into enthusiastic applause. Alex looked from Commander Rudge to Jeff and from Jeff to Ben. Ben's face was a picture of dismay. He leaned across to Callie and Alex. 'He's made a mistake,' he whispered. He turned to appeal to Jeff.

By way of reply Jeff rose from his seat and walked round to Ben's chair. He handed him his crutches. 'If you're joining the SESU, Ben, you'd better get it straight now. The head of the SESU does not make mistakes – ever!' His face split into a wide grin, completely transforming him from the cool Jeff they had known. In that moment Alex was sure that Jeff had never intended to harm Ben or any of them. There had to be a reasonable explanation for what Alex had seen on the overhang. Jeff reached down to help Ben up from his seat. 'Congratulations, Cadet Ortlund. But get a move on. You're keeping everyone waiting.'

As Ben hesitantly hobbled towards the podium on his crutches, the applause doubled in volume. Alex watched him making his steady progress without the least hint of pride, and felt a lump in his throat. He wasn't sure why Ben had been awarded the SESU place, but he glimpsed something in him now that must somehow have come through in the testing periods of the race – a quiet strength and a deep reservoir of courage. Ben would make his way up steadily through the ranks of SESU, leaving a legacy of creative, productive projects that no one, apart from those working alongside him, would ever know had originated with him.

Alex watched as Ben balanced with one crutch to shake hands with Commander Rudge. He was surprised at the insight he had just been given and then startled by a second insight. His vision of how Ben was, and how he would be, was a gift. It had helped Alex to see the race and the winning of the place in the SESU in perspective. He wasn't as ready to benefit from the place as Ben was. His father's words suddenly came back to him.

'You have many gifts and talents. The SESU might

be the right place for you to use them. Or you might be better off using them somewhere else.' And what was it he had said before that? 'It doesn't matter if you lose, Alex. God has a plan for your life.'

God has a plan for your life.

The words hit Alex as if they had been built six foot high in neon lights and a thrill of elation ran through him. He had a lot to find out about this God. But it was going to be good, he was sure of it. It was going to be, he thought with a leap of joy, the best thing that had ever happened to him.

Alex felt sure this revelation had transformed him. He looked at Callie to see if she had noticed anything. Callie had her eyes fixed on Ben. A smile of pride and joy lifted her lips and shone in her eyes. Tears streamed down her face. She was clapping so hard Alex thought her arms might snap.

Commander Rudge had been having a few quiet words with Ben. Whatever he said seemed to reassure Ben, for he was now smiling broadly. Commander Rudge held up his hand for silence. 'Ladies and gentlemen, in a few moments we will be enjoying the delicious banquet which has been prepared for us in Ben's honour. But, before we do so, our worthy winner, Ben Ortlund, has a few things he wants to say to us.'

The buzz of noise in the room dropped to an immediate hush as Ben took his place behind the microphone.

'First of all, I want to say that I don't really feel I deserve this.'

Typical, Alex thought.

'But I feel very proud and honoured to be chosen – especially when I think about some of the competitors I'm supposed to have beaten. I want to thank two of them especially because they've been good friends –

111

and because they saved my life.' Ben paused as a thought struck him. He looked round till he located that table where Seth and Ricky were sitting. 'And I'd like to thank Ricky for all he did to rescue me too.'

Ricky stared stonily back. There was a moment of embarrassment as someone started to applaud, only to find that no one was joining in. But Ben did something which showed Alex more clearly than any words why he was a winner. He hobbled across to the nearest table, propped his crutches against it, leaned against a chair to support himself and began applauding Ricky himself.

For a moment Alex was stupefied. Then he joined in, Callie applauding alongside him. Whatever else Ricky had done, he had helped to save Ben's life. The whole room soon burst into applause. If some of it was for the gesture Ben had made, that didn't matter. Alex saw the slow smile on Ricky's face before he bent his head to hide it.

Ben stayed where he was to finish his speech. His voice carried clearly across the now quiet room. 'There are two good reasons why I'd like to ask my friends Alex and Callie to join me now. One is so that you can show them your appreciation with a round of applause. The other is so that they can help me back onto my crutches!'

A ripple of laughter circulated the room, to be followed by a renewed burst of clapping and cheering as Alex and Callie joined Ben. Together they walked back to their table. Alex thought he couldn't have felt happier if he had won himself. No. He qualified the thought. Tonight had been an enriching experience he would have missed out on if he had won.

Commander Rudge had one last word to say. 'And now, if you're not too exhausted from all that applauding, we'll eat. I'm sure there'll be a chance to talk to Ben and the others later. Meantime – enjoy yourselves!'

A happy burst of chatter and laughter spread across the dining-room as the first course of soup was served. To Alex's surprise Commander Rudge made his way across to their table.

The Commander's first words as he seated himself next to Jeff made Alex smile. 'I thought I'd sit with you, if you don't mind, because you're probably the only people in the room who aren't curious as to why Seth and Ricky were disqualified from the race, and why Jeff is in SESU uniform. You're not curious, are you?'

Callie laughed. 'Not in the least curious,' she said.

'I'm very curious!' Alex remarked, smiling. 'In fact there are several things I would like to know, Commander Rudge.'

'Are there indeed?' Commander Rudge held Alex's gaze levelly for a moment, then a hint of humour kindled in his grey eyes. 'I think we can promise you enough answers to make your head spin before the end of the evening, Alex. But we'll just take one thing at a time.' He turned to Ben. 'What about you, Ben? Did you wonder why Jeff was in SESU uniform tonight?'

'No,' Ben replied with a slow smile. 'I think I know already.'

Jeff looked thoughtfully at Ben. 'All right. Why am I in SESU uniform then?'

All eyes were fixed on Ben, waiting for his answer. But Alex looked at Commander Rudge. His face was carefully expressionless as he watched Ben. This was the man, thought Alex, who had all the real answers, and he wondered what secrets were about to be brought out into the open.

Chapter fifteen

'Why am I in SESU uniform, Ben?' Jeff repeated.

Ben was smiling. Alex suspected that he was enjoying the moment of suspense he had created. Ben shrugged his shoulders.

'Because you're obviously already a member of the SESU,' he said.

'Then why was I in the race?'

'You weren't.'

Alex caught Callie's eye. They exchanged glances of surprise. Jeff merely smiled.

'You were placed there,' Ben continued, 'to keep an eye on things because Commander Rudge suspected there might be some cheating.'

Commander Rudge nodded. 'All of you won your places fairly, or so it seemed. I had a feeling though that there was something going on that I didn't know about. I wasn't sure which of you might cause trouble, so the best idea was to send Jeff along and hope he would see the signs when whoever it was gave themselves away.'

Alex was surer than ever now that there was a reasonable explanation for Jeff's being with the Rock Man when he started the avalanche. He knew that he wouldn't concentrate on the other explanations until he had this clear in his mind. So, taking advantage of a lull in the conversation as a waitress came to clear their empty soup bowls away, he plucked up the courage to ask the question that had been disturbing him for so long.

'Commander, there's something I'd like to ask Jeff to clear up before we go any further.'

'Go ahead,' invited the Commander.

Alex decided to launch into his question without preamble. 'What were you doing with that Rock Man when he started the avalanche, Jeff?'

'Trying to stop him,' Jeff replied promptly.

Jeff's explanation was so obvious that it made Alex feel like a fool.

Jeff went on to explain that the Rock Men, who had always kept their distance from the rest of the community, had recently been acting strangely. Members of the SESU had reported Rock Men spying on them; provisions had disappeared and equipment had been damaged.

The Rock Men, for reasons of their own, were only too happy to help Ricky win the race. The general plan was that they would do whatever they could to stop or delay the other candidates. There were some deliberate traps set up beforehand, but they also hoped to have unexpected opportunities during the race. Placing themselves at strategic points on Anderloss was one of the things planned beforehand by Ricky and the Rock Men.

'The supposed radio message you had from Base, Alex, was an example of something planned partly in advance,' explained Jeff. 'They had equipment ready if the opportunity arose. Ricky had probably just left one of the Rock Men in hiding when he spotted you in the snow-drift. It was easy enough for him to make contact with him before he fetched Callie to rescue you. He didn't really want anything bad to happen to you. He just wanted the coast clear for himself. He thought that Callie was no threat but that you were, Alex. He probably told one of the Rock Men to radio before the three of you started climbing.'

Jeff went on to say that he had begun to suspect Ricky was the trouble-maker when they were at the caves. When he had set out to find his spaceship to help Seth, he had seen Ricky talking to a Rock Man. The radio message that he need not go back for Seth had freed him to keep an eye on Ricky, but by then he had no idea where Ricky was. All he could do was watch at the foot of Anderloss.

Jeff was lucky enough to be in the right place at the right time. He had seen Ricky arrive with the Rock Man, and thought the pair of them might have had time to set a trap or two while he had been waiting for them, but there was nothing Jeff could do. The only choice he had was to follow either Ricky or the Rock Man. He had followed the Rock Man, but it was not until he had come out onto the overhang that Jeff realised what he intended to do, and he had been seconds too late to stop him.

'I could have told you the last part,' Ben said quietly to Callie and Alex. Alex threw Callie an exasperated look. They had not confided their doubts to Ben because they had not wanted to worry him!

'I saw what happened from higher up the mountain. I saw Jeff tackle the Rock Man and went to his help. But I didn't see the second Rock Man who attacked me from behind and forced me to the edge of the overhang.

'The Rock Man I was dealing with turned out to be a tough fighter. He knocked me out cold,' Jeff said ruefully. By the time I came round there was no sign of him or his friend. Ben had disappeared too. I didn't realise till later that he had been pushed over the edge. When I looked at the slope below I couldn't spot anyone. The only person I did see was higher up the mountain and, thinking of the condition I had last seen him in, I was rather surprised.

'Seth!' exclaimed Callie.

'That's right,' confirmed Jeff.

'But Seth was unconscious in my spaceship,' Alex protested.

'Well, apparently he recovered well enough to climb Anderloss!' Jeff amended. 'I'm not too sure how much Seth Morcombe pulled the wool over our eyes. When he was ill back in the caves, I don't know how much of that was genuine.'

'That's something we'll find out,' commented Commander Rudge grimly. 'We realised quite early on that Seth was secretly taking drugs to give him that extra edge. After he was almost caught with them in the cavern and threw them away, he began to get edgy. His thinking got muddled and in the end he was forced into actions he wouldn't normally have taken, like trying to take over your ship, Alex, and replacing Ricky's flag on the summit with his own.'

Alex nodded. Seth's actions began to make sense now. One thing puzzled him though. 'So it was the drugs that Seth threw into the pool that made it burst into flame?' It seemed a perfectly reasonable guess. Alex was rather taken aback when Jeff and Commander Rudge broke into helpless laughter. He turned to Callie questioningly but she was as puzzled as he was.

'Alex,' Jeff managed at last. 'It was a chemical Ricky dropped in.' He went on to explain that it was one of the many tricks and traps Ricky had set up in the Waste Zone.

'What exactly did Ricky do?' asked Callie. 'Apart from getting the Rock Men to do his dirty work for him.'

It appeared that Ricky was under tremendous pressure from his parents to win the place in the SESU. They would have bought it for him if they could. One thing in Ricky's favour was that he did have a realistic understanding of his abilities. He knew he couldn't win the place fairly. The only alternative was to bribe the Rock Men to help him cheat.

'But I don't think, to be fair to him,' emphasised Commander Rudge, 'that he thought anybody would get seriously hurt. He planned the traps to delay people. I think when he saw what happened to Ben on the mountain he was genuinely concerned.'

'Things got a bit out of control, did they?' asked Alex.

'I don't think he ever had them properly under control,' explained the Commander. 'It's obvious now that he was never SESU material. The whole idea was badly organised from the start.'

Alex thought back to the things that had gone wrong – the call on his radio which had taken him off the track, and the trap in which Ben's leg had been caught. He wondered about the time he had lost consciousness in the cave. Ricky had brought him round.

'Those caverns?' he asked. 'How did we all come to arrive there at the same time?'

It was Jeff who spoke this time. 'You shouldn't have. That was an instance of Ricky's plans going badly wrong. He and the Rock Men laid traps that nobody fell into as well as some that worked. A few of the Rock Men were worried about what the others were doing and warned me a couple of times, and sometimes the traps didn't work anyway. They just delayed people so that everyone arrived at the caverns together. This stopped them trapping anyone effectively in the caves. It would have been easier to deal with people one at a time.

'I wonder if Ricky tried to deal with me?' mused Alex. 'I don't know how I got knocked out. It could have been Ricky, but it doesn't make sense that he stayed there to bring me round.'

'Would it make more sense if I told you he saw me coming up the tunnel towards you both?'

Alex looked sharply at Jeff. 'Yes,' he said and shivered slightly. So Ricky had been Kensa, the Boss Man, who had set the traps. 'Jeff!' Alex added as another piece of puzzle slotted into place. 'Did you say some of the Rock Men warned you?'

'Yes. Why?' asked Jeff.

'Because,' replied Alex, remembering, 'one of them came looking for you on Ricky's ship by mistake.' He told them about his encounter with the frightened little Rock Man.

Jeff grimaced. 'Yes. Ship-master. That's me. Don't ask me why. Sounds like you met Jongjo. I'd better explain what happened to him. And thank him.'

Callie was still thinking of their experience in the caverns. 'Those caves were dreadful,' she said shuddering. 'Why did you send us there at all?'

'Ricky's fault again,' Commander Rudge said. Before he could explain, the next course arrived – meat in a savoury sauce, accompanied by bowls of steaming vegetables. The questions and answers continued to ricochet across the table as the meat was served and the vegetables passed round. Then Commander Rudge returned to Callie's question.

120

'You'll have to revisit the caverns sometime, Callie,' he commented with a twinkle in his eye.

'No way!' protested Callie.

Commander Rudge laughed. 'No, seriously. You'll like it. We're building a fabulous new leisure complex there, complete with hot springs and a converted rock pool for swimming. Ricky took down the signs so that you all entered the old part of the caverns which haven't been developed yet.'

There was so much to piece together now they knew Ricky was behind it all, but as they arrived at the sweet course – a frothy concoction of mousse, fruit and ice-cream – Commander Rudge drew a halt to the questions.

'Alex, Callie,' he began, looking at their faces in turn searchingly, 'I've something I want to say to you.'

Alex tensed under the Commander's penetrating gaze. He was going to be taken to task for all the things he had done wrong. With a sinking feeling in the pit of his stomach, he waited for the Commander's next words.

'You haven't shown any sign of disappointment, either of you, at not winning the race, though I imagine you are disappointed. Since Ricky was disqualified the first place could have gone to any of the three of you. Both of you, Alex and Callie, did things which would have made you worthy members of a SESU team. The reason that, when it came to choosing, the place went to Ben, was because he entered the race with a terrific handicap. He probably should not have taken part at all.'

Alex's initial feeling of relief was placed by curiosity. He stole a glance at Ben, intrigued. Ben was looking down, seemingly studying his dessert spoon.

'Ben Ortlund is one of the brightest students in his academic year. He is also one of the best all round sportsmen. Not the best kind of competitor to have against you in a race.'

Alex took another sideways glance at Ben. This new information didn't seem to tie in with Ben's performance in the race. Ben suddenly looked up and caught Alex's eye. He raised his eyebrows in the kind of expression Alex used himself when his mother was singing his praises to one of her friends. Alex smiled, and Ben smiled back.

'But, as I said, Ben entered the race with a handicap. He is only just recovering from a spacecraft accident in which he sustained heavy injuries rescuing his co-pilot. I think you'll agree that Ben's performance in this race under those circumstances was quite something.'

'It would have been my last performance at anything if Alex and Callie hadn't saved my life,' put in Ben.

'If you're protesting, Ben, that you don't feel it's right to take the SESU place when they get nothing,' said Commander Rudge evenly, 'don't worry about it. I've got something lined up for Alex and Callie which will make every bit as good use of their exceptional talents.'

Alex and Callie looked at each other, then eagerly back at Commander Rudge. Alex felt as if a weight had been lifted from him. It seemed all his earlier worries had been for nothing. 'God has a plan for your life,' Alex thought and the excitement bubbled up inside him.

'What is it?' Callie asked curiously.

'The leisure complex at the Stopping Place is only part of a huge plan for the redevelopment of the Waste Zone. And this incidentally, is what started the trouble with the Rock Men. They thought that if we were taking over the Waste Zone, the next thing we might do would be to drive them out of their homes in the hill country on its northern border. Their aim was to make the Waste Zone seem a dangerous place so we would leave it alone. I don't know whose idea it was to work together, the Rock Men's or Ricky's, but his desire to win the race tied in beautifully with their plans. It took little encouragement from Ricky to make the Rock Men try to sabotage the race for the other competitors whenever they could.

'As soon as we found all this out we set up some talks with the Rock Men. It'll take a while to put their minds at ease, but I hope eventually they'll feel as enthusiastic as I think you will when I tell you what we're doing with the Waste Zone.

'We're turning it into a training ground with special courses for students from all over the galaxy. They'll be trained for the SESU as well as for other fields. There will be senior tutors – experts in different areas – in charge, but they will need skilled, adaptable assistants to help them. Interested?'

The meal was over and their table was soon swamped with well-wishers congratulating Ben, but praising Alex and Callie too. When the crowds began to thin out, Commander Rudge drew Alex aside.

'I'm glad you've accepted that place, Alex,' he said. 'It seems like history repeating itself.'

Alex looked at him bemused.

'I mean your father,' the Commander went on. 'He had a chance to be on the SESU team the year after I joined. I think, with his unusual gifts, he would have been in my shoes now if he had taken the place. He volunteered instead for pioneering work, setting up a model settlement. I think you can be proud, Alex, of following in his footsteps.'

Alex was glad that the Commander didn't seem to expect any reply. He patted Alex on the back and walked away. Alex stood looking across the room where his father was talking animatedly with a group of cadets. He felt suddenly very proud of him.

A light touch on his arm brought him out of his reflection with a start. It was Callie.

'Well, Alex, what do you think?' she asked, her eyes brimming with excitement. 'Isn't it like a dream come true!'

'You know what I think it's like?' he answered, tucking her arm into his. 'It's like opening a door you thought wouldn't lead anywhere in particular, and finding it opens out into a whole new world full of wonderful things and amazing adventures.'

'Wow,' said Callie softly. 'You're right. I can see it too. Alex, did you know you're quite a poet!'

Alex laughed. 'Maybe I am. Maybe I'm a lot of things I don't know about yet. I know one thing I am, despite the fact that tonight should have proved I'm not . . .'

'One thing you're not, Alex, is clever enough to think of a riddle to outsmart me!' retorted Callie smiling. 'You feel like a winner. I know. I feel like a winner too!'

Alex looked at her in amazement. 'Yes. That *is* how I feel – like a winner! And it's a great feeling.'

A winner not of the race to Anderloss, he thought, but of something better. Something that could not quite be put into words. Something to do with his discovery that there was a God who cared.

He smiled down at Callie who had helped him make that discovery. 'Come on,' he said. 'Let's go and join the others. We're all invited back to Ben's house to celebrate and we wouldn't want to be the last ones there.'

'No,' smiled Callie, letting Alex guide her to where their parents and friends were talking and laughing with Ben and his family. 'We wouldn't want to be last!'

Some other Leopard Books for you to read:

Stranded!
Cathie Bartlam
Ian puts all he can into learning to waterski but though it looks easy, the reality is different. During the Lake District holiday Ian makes some unexpected discoveries about his cousins and himself, especially when he is the centre of a dramatic rescue.

The Key of Zorgen
Lynette Bishop
The key takes Robert and Debbie into the kingdom of Mondar which is in a different time from ours. They meet Kate and her strange cat, Mig, and are drawn into a desperate attempt to protect the key of the kingdom from Dolan, the king's enemy.

Roughshod Ride
Gail Vinall
Zena and Toni are suspicious about the stable manager but lack proof. Why is Cheri suddenly lame and why does Steve lose his job at the stables? Zena and Toni are up against a clever schemer.

Hawkeye of Paradise Row
The Paradise Row Gang
Hawkeye hits the Jackpot
Veronica Heley
Three books about Toby, Nikki and their friends. They fight neighbourhood crime, help to pull together the kids in the area into a community and tackle the problem of game machine addiction. Three exciting and realistic stories.